On Kelsey Creek

On Kelsey Creek

Phyllis Whetstone Taper

The Conservation Press
Oakland, California

Published by
THE CONSERVATION PRESS
Berkeley Creators Association Educational Foundation
1170 Powell Street, Oakland, CA 94608

Distributed by
BORED FEET PRESS
Post Office Box 1832, Mendocino, CA 95460
www.boredfeet.com

Cover photograph copyright © 2004 by Robin Mark Freeman
Book and cover design by Nancy Austin

Publisher's Cataloging in Publication Data:

Taper, Phyllis

On Kelsey Creek
/Phyllis Whetstone Taper -- 1st ed.
224 p. ; 23 cm.

ISBN: 0-9762362-1-4

I. Title

PS3539.A519606 2004

Second printing, January 2005

For my family and to my brother Bill.

Thanks to: Bob Gluck, and his writing group;
Robin Freeman and Nancy Austin for more writing and production;
Richard Schwarzenberger, Robbie Brandwynne, and Leanne Hinton
for proofreading, and Judy Hardin, resourceful and helpful in all ways.

Phyllis Whetstone Taper
Kensington 2004

CALIFORNIA, 1927

Chapter 1

Charlie was running late, but he cut the last bits of meat from his thin T-bone steak and pushed his coffee cup forward for a refill, anyway. With the fan circling deliberately on the ceiling and the green blinds drawn, the cafe had an underwater look—you could almost imagine it was cool in here. He fished absently for the Bull Durham sack in his shirt pocket, but gladly accepted an Old Gold from the hop farmer on the stool next to him. Anybody who said ready-made cigarettes weren't better than hand-rolled was kidding himself.

He pictured Giorgio over the grade in Kelseyville, anxious to get the shake piled in Charlie's truck made into boxes for the pear season, though that wouldn't even start for a week, two, more likely. Then everybody would be lining up jobs, fruit tramps would be rolling into town to grab the best camp sites and get set up. But Giorgio would worry till he had a mountain of boxes made up long before the first pear was picked. It was a waste, like getting up two hours before breakfast. Charlie tossed a dollar on the counter and waved away the change.

Outside, the sun hit him straight down as a jackhammer. The street had a bleached out noon-day look like an old sepia photograph. Time seemed at a standstill.

A block ahead by the train station, Charlie could see a small blonde man standing beside the tracks with his suitcase, though the white dots of steam from the train's departing toot were widening and fading in the sky. Charlie hurried to get the truck going. Even if the guy was a crook or a halfwit, it would be better to have his company than to run the grade alone again.

"Going into Lake County?" he asked pleasantly when he drew up beside him. "Better hop in. The next bus is tomorrow."

The young man looked up smiling as he pushed his brown cardboard suitcase ahead of him onto the cab floor. "Thanks! This place looks pretty forsaken. I'm Irv Moody."

Charlie nodded. He gunned the engine and the truck ground heavily upward through steep hills mottled with clumps of dusty chaparral. Irv leaned close to the windshield to trace the surging curves of the tawny hills against the deep blue sky. Low-domed live oaks brooded their dark shadows. Some of the chemise bore small heads of blossom already shriveled and brown. Here and there a few swaying branches pointed fingers of lavender bloom.

Though Irv was aching for sleep, the hot, scented air stung him wide awake. He followed the sidewise sweep of a hawk across the sky, and felt almost like he was soaring up there himself, leaving all the crap like his job at the country club and the sad stuff at home back on a whole different plane.

Charlie, watching him, could hardly believe the elation he saw on Irv's face. "Do you know somebody in Kelseyville?" he asked. He was afraid this little man didn't know what he was in for.

Irv nodded. "The Wintons. You know where their place is?"

"Sure do," Charlie said. "Our places are both up Kelsey Creek."

Irv glanced at Charlie. He seemed friendly, but he looked real glum and his voice had a sarcastic cut to it as though he might blow up easily.

"Bill Winton and I went all through high school together in Oakland. I sure hope Pod's health is better up here, like they thought it would be. Bill and I call him Pod, like padre in Spanish," Irv explained.

They rode through a long barren stretch where the wind blew the hot smell of tar weed and sage into the cab along with a cloud of red dust. Irv gradually sagged forward, asleep, with the dust rimming his nostrils and deep patterns of sweat darkening his blue shirt. His blond hair clung to his forehead in wet streaks. There, Irv, Charlie thought, now you look more like Lake County.

You might have known he would be going to the Winton's. Charlie thought. Frankly, he was afraid Wint wasn't going to make a go of ranching. Almost every time he went over there, Wint would have the tractor or the truck apart, trying to fix it before he could begin the day's work, looking exhausted already. Or take the day he and Bill were waiting for Wint to bring the team out for the spray rig they were going to use on both their places. Suddenly they had heard big jolting thumps and whinnying threats, Wint hollering and swearing, sounding feeble compared to the horses. Then he came flying through the barn door as though he had been tossed out with a pitchfork, and sat there on the manure pile, gray in the face, struggling to get his breath. Finally, when he could breathe, he looked down at himself and gave a sort of laugh, as though he accepted the judgment. Charlie knew how he felt. It was pretty much a stand-off which was worse—to have your animals or your machinery turn against you. He decided machinery was. At least, when you kicked a horse, he knew what you meant.

The truck was balking at the climb now, almost stalling till he shifted into low. If he had a decent piece of machinery under him, he could run the grade in a quarter of the time it took him in this worn-out wreck. Hinkley had bought his wife a fancy Marmon; why he refused to get better equipment for the business was beyond him. Probably, it was because he was sure old Charlie would put up with driving this decrepit excuse for a truck year after year. Hinkley had him by the balls and wasn't going to let go.

It was Hinkley that complained. You wouldn't think it was possible for the pear crop off the orchard to be smaller and worth less every year, but it was. Maybe it was the soil, but more likely it was because he never was cut out to be a farmer, Charlie admitted privately. The only thing that flourished was Viv's rabbits. They multiplied beyond belief. He might have to start taking care of the rabbits himself to get the population under control. He hated the rabbits, but he had to admit they fed the family when his pay was short, which was most of the time.

He and Viv had felt so good when old man Hinkley suggested they move to the pretty little ranch when they first got married. For rent, just give him part of the crop when it came in, he said. Have a real farm to raise kids on. What actually happened was that he'd become Hinkley's captive hired hand, on the spot whenever Hinkley needed him, come what may.

It had been a nice place till everything got run down. Now, the doors and gates sagged. The little green lawn in front of the house had gone to tufts and patches, the ruts in the driveway were deeper and the puddles lasted longer. The keg hoop he had put up on the barn for fun the day they moved in sagged crooked and red with rust. And people still called it the Hinkley place.

He remembered the day they first moved in. He'd nailed the hoop up so he and the guys helping him could shoot baskets. Vivian ran to explore every corner, quick as a child, her eyes blazing blue the way they got. They parked the dining table under the big oak and had a picnic on it outside, danced to Rudy Vallee as soon as the radio was hooked up. That was before the rabbits.

Irv started in his seat, blinking and then opening his eyes wide, though Charlie could tell he didn't wake up enough to really see anything. His eyes were almost as blue as Vivian's except they were like blue enamel, where you could see right into Vivian's, like jewels. Not that he spent time gazing into Viv's eyes now.

The truck ground on and on, the hills tossing up around him like billows. Irv was asleep again with a beatified look on his face. Charlie imagined shaking him and shouting, "Come on, Irv, wake up!" but he didn't have the heart to do it really.

The monotonous tittering and squealing of the shakes he was hauling might have made him sleepy too, if it didn't annoy him so much. It had sounded almost cheerful at first, but it got to seem nagging and persistent mile after mile. It reminded him of the load of screaming kids on the old school bus. No wonder old man Snook who drove it hated kids so much he would hit chuck holes on purpose so he could watch the little ones bouncing like fleas in his rear view mirror.

He was beginning to get the familiar ache in his solar plexus again, as if loneliness was sitting hunched up inside him, though he wasn't even alone this time. Irv might be asleep but he was still there, snoring innocently. Charlie looked over at him, wondering how he had gotten the purplish darkness under his eyes. He didn't look like a big dissipater or anything, but you could tell by the way he slept that he really needed it.

He swung the truck around another curve into the sun. Just off the side of the road in a small clearing, a turkey buzzard hunched its wings and pushed its legs forward to land next to a gray-brown carcass another bird was already pulling strings of guts out of. The buzzard went to work on it without even glancing at the truck. Charlie honked peevishly. All they had to do for a living was pick it up. Then when they wanted to, they could go up the sky as though they were in an elevator, just by setting their wings. They could soar right down to Mexico when they got tired of the U.S.A. Like Giorgio and Gloria. They had gone to Mexico. They had even sailed to Hawaii. Slick little dago knew how to make money, and now he'd got Gloria trained to do it too, packing pears. He hated to think what the two of them made in a day, it would make him sick. The thing that kept him chained to Hinkley was that hauling was a year-round job, and there weren't all that many in Kelseyville, unless you owned a store or something. He didn't own a goddamn thing, except a flivver, and didn't see how he ever would.

It was an hour before Irv woke up again. He shook his head to clear it, and sat up and looked out the window. They were just pulling around a long curve, and suddenly there it was, far below the reaching arc of sky, the broad valley slowly wheeling into view, and the lake stretching silvery blue along the north. Konocti, the big mountain almost violet with distance, was settled like a sleeping lion at the southeast end, its crater worn to a swale. It rose high above the hills that ringed the valley. Dark orchard rows crisscrossed the valley floor. A white road threaded through them, dead straight for a ways, then making right angle turns that respected old grant divisions. A smudged line of trees and bushes showed where the creek wound down to the lake.

The whole valley seemed to be looking to Konocti, waiting. Irv let his head swivel from one side to the other to get the full scope of it. "Jesus," he whispered.

Charlie didn't want to hear about how pretty Lake County was. "Let's take a break," he said brusquely. The tall load tilted as he eased the truck onto the turnout. When he turned off the motor the silence seemed pure, absolute. They both got down from the cab stiffly. Charlie turned his head half away from the valley, giving it a sidelong glance.

Irv scrambled up to the top of the bank. "It looks like some kind of promised land," he said.

Charlie stood below with his back to the view, watching his urine drill a dark hole in the powdery dust. As they climbed back in the truck Charlie asked, "You don't get carsick, do you? It's just as crooked going down as it was coming up, and a whole lot faster."

"No I'm O.K., just sleepy. I've been working nights a lot since I got laid off. A lot of people have been laid off in Oakland."

"That right?" Charlie said.

"Yes. Just when everything seemed rosy."

"I know what you mean," Charlie said.

"That's why I came up to see Bill now. He wrote me there was plenty of work in Lake County, on account of the fruit season." He sat rigidly straight for a short while before he slumped back to sleep.

When he woke they were running through pear orchards on the flat valley floor. Tall oaks along the roadside cast shadows so sharp they could feel the cool edge as they entered them. They made good time now on the straightaway, slowing only briefly for the sharp turns.

At one of the crossroads Charlie pulled to an abrupt stop at the side of the road, facing a small horse and wagon stopped at the opposite corner. Irv could see that someone in a blue shirt or dress was bent over double on the wagon seat. Charlie got out quickly, calling "Beulah? Are you O.K?" Irv followed him.

A big young woman raised herself up.

"Oh, yes. Hello, Charlie. I'm fine." An innocent smile showing strong teeth spaced with small gaps spread on her long face. Irv found himself smiling back.

"This is Irv, Beulah. He's come up from Oakland to visit Bill Winton."

"Pleased to meet you," she said, holding out two plums iced with silvery bloom. "Have a plum." Charlie took them and handed one to Irv. Juice spurted when they bit into them. Irv wiped his chin with a handkerchief, and Charlie pulled the back of his hand across his mouth.

"Mm, good," he mumbled around a mouthful.

"I was taking some to Muriel at the library, but I spilled them all over." The purple fruit was scattered thick on the floor boards under the wagon seat. Charlie went around to the opposite side and gathered them, brushing off the worst of the dirt as he filled the basket.

"Do you know the direction to town all right, now?"

Beulah looked around, confused. Then she pointed to the right, raising pale blue eyes to Charlie for confirmation.

"There you go, Beulah. Tell your dad and Ernie 'hello' for me, will you?"

Charlie took the corner slowly, watching the wagon in his rear view. "They'll be O.K." he told Irv, "The horse knows the way."

Irv was amazed at how the look on Charlie's face changed him. He hadn't realized what a good-looking guy Charlie was: curly lashes and clear gray eyes, easy smile. Different as day from night when he wasn't so gloomy. And now he was relaxed you could see how big he was, though he didn't act conscious of his size the way a lot did.

They were running through walnut groves now on both sides of the road, their shade dark as water under great branches almost meeting between the rows. Neither spoke for a long while. When they reached a wide stretch of gravel and started to edge down into the almost dry creek bed, Charlie said, "This is where I unload." The fruit shed, faced with crimped galvanized siding, stood isolated behind a high mesh fence in a field of dry grass on the far bank. It was box shaped, businesslike. The only sound, beside the shrilling grasshoppers, was a thin, clear din of hammering coming from one corner.

Chapter 2

Giorgio was alone at the shed, working at a bench at the edge of a loading platform. Brads were lined up in a feeder so he could pick them up with his hammer, and a small stack of shakes was in reach before him. His movements were without flourish, almost secretive, the sound of the pine wood scraping across the workbench as he turned shakes into boxes was deliberate and peaceful, like brush strokes on a drum. He had an aloof, brooding air, wore a fine white shirt and black trousers, and had stayed neat and clean all day long, except for the pine dust that gilded the folds of his clothing and settled on his eyebrows. Giorgio never seemed to hurry, but it was said he had made twenty-seven dollars one day. That was more than the fastest packers could earn. Charlie stood by, watching silently.

A blue Star roadster with its top down came through the gate and nosed up to the platform beside Giorgio's red Oldsmobile. Gloria was Georgio's wife now, but back in their high school days, when Charlie was a hero, she'd been a special clowning buddy in the elaborate gags he cooked up to divert himself and the school. She waved, then reached a slim arm out for cigarettes and lighter. She looked as cool and assured as Giorgio himself as she settled to smoke and wait. Charlie turned away after raising his hand in return. He'd almost rather run into somebody he owed money to than an old admirer. He felt like a fool standing there waiting for Giorgio to recognize his existence.

"Charlie," Giorgio said, with a polite nod after he had finished.

Charlie nodded, holding his lips tight together, as though he too were preoccupied. "This is Irv." His voice sounded almost like a growl, and he had to clear his throat to finish. "He'll help unload." Irv, watching, decided Charlie was about the most changeable person he had ever seen.

Giorgio climbed quickly onto the truck, loosened the ropes, and began sending bundles of shakes down to the other two. Irv passed them to Charlie to stack.

For a while Giorgio's rhythm carried Charlie along. It eased his back and cancelled his thoughts. Then suddenly he jerked upright breaking the chain. Whose goddamned job was this anyway, he thought. He planted his hands on the truck bed and hauled himself up on it beside Giorgio. "I'll handle this end," he said gruffly.

"O.K.," Giorgio said, jumping down to change places with him. Charlie launched a few bundles at Giorgio's rate. It felt rushed, unnatural. He resented the way Giorgio had tossed the shakes around, like it was recess, taking liberties, somehow. As he turned for a bundle, pain streaked through him as if he had grabbed a live wire. Jerkily, he sat down on the truck bed.

"Shit," he said bleakly.

Giorgio and Irv unloaded the truck while Charlie sat trying to straighten his spine out along the edge of a door frame. He got up slowly when Giorgio asked if he wanted a ride home. "I can drive all right," he said, and turned toward the truck. The second step he took, his leg seemed not to be there, and he crumbled toward Irv walking beside him. Irv caught him around the waist and held on desperately to keep him from crashing till Giorgio got to him too. They walked him to the truck between them.

"Why don't I drive," Irv said. Charlie stood by the door a second; his legs seemed all right but his heart was pounding so hard he could hardly hear anything else.

"You can if you want," he said at last, and let them walk him around to the rider's side. Gloria sat watching. It seemed like a mile around the truck. Beads of sweat springing out on his forehead felt like insects landing on it.

Irv drove without talking, carefully avoiding bumps and sharp moves until Charlie felt like shouting, "For Christ's sake, just drive. I'm all right." It made it seem farther than it was, Irv babying him like that. He slowed to a crawl when Charlie told him to pull into the driveway to his house, but the truck bounced noisily over the deep ruts.

A woman ran out the door of the house as soon as Irv had helped Charlie out of the rider's side of the cab. She held her skirt and apron up with both hands so she could hurry, and the heavy knot of hazelnut-colored hair slipped and loosened as she ran, so that curly strands frayed out around her face. She looked tanned and sturdy, and a little worn, but her dark blue eyes, flaring with anxiety, were so beautiful Irv stood staring, when he should have been reassuring her Charlie would live.

"Oh, Charlie, what did you do?" she cried.

"I didn't 'do' anything, dammit, My back went out on me when I was unloading,"

"Gee, don't jump on me! I didn't do anything either. You scared me." She was half laughing.

Charlie glared at her. "Funny, huh?"

"Oh, you goof, I'm just glad you're not hurt."

Irv wanted to tell Charlie he was blind if he couldn't see that much, but he just pulled his suitcase out of the truck and stood holding it. Charlie started to limp off toward the house, then turned back. "Oh. Irv, I'm sorry, this is Vivian. Irv's come up to visit Bill Winton."

She smiled at Irv. "I'll drive you on in the Ford then. Why don't you just lie down awhile, Charlie, and give your back a chance to unwind."

During dinner, chicken and dumplings with fresh peas, which Charlie had to admit was not only better than rabbit, but good, the children annoyed him. Rob kept asking why would his back do that, with four-year-old persistence, and Isobel looked sad and kept her eyes on her plate for the whole meal after he snapped there was nothing for her to be sorry about when she said "I'm sorry, Papa." He felt like a shit.

He took a hot bath to see if that would help, lowering himself into the tub carefully, teeth bared in a prepared wince. Soon bumps of muscle in his neck and shoulders began to ease out, his face drooped sober and sad, and for a long while he sat staring beyond his knees, one hand sympathetically cupping his genitals. He thought he would try to figure his life out, but dropped off to sleep.

A half hour later he came out to the kitchen with a white towel tucked around his waist. His face and arms, where he was tanned, had a rosy glow instead of the mustard tinge he had come home with, and his hair clustered into damp curls. Viv shook her head and laughed, "Well, at least you look like you feel better." She got another towel to put around his shoulders and laid her head against his back with her arms around him. "Don't get a chill or you'll be worse off than ever," she said.

She sounded like his grandmother. As he turned to tell her so, a muscle under his shoulder blade twitched, threatening to clench up. He swore and bent over, crossed his arms on his chest, and shuffled back to the bedroom to flop on the bed again.

The sound of voices in the kitchen woke him. Isobel's and another young girl's voice, Jeanne Winton, come to pick up Izzy for Christian Endeavor. Then Viv hurrying Izzy, telling her to take a sweater—it could turn cool. Then Irv's voice came through, asking "How is Charlie's back feeling now?" and Bill Winton's, "We're going to listen to the fights in town. If Charlie feels up to it, we could park so he can hear from the car."

Charlie had forgotten the fights. He rolled over onto his back to consider. Every ring fan in Big Valley would be there, even those who had pretty good radio sets at home would come in to hear the broadcast over the big morning-glory speakers Roy Robison had put up on the hardware store roof for sports events. Main Street would be crawling with cars as fans tried to find parking near to the store as possible. The speakers would blare on and on with the introductions; arguments and bets on the street would run high, though if any bet was more than ten dollars everybody would know it was a joke.

Charlie turned on his side to ease himself out of bed and appeared at the door in his bathrobe. "You convinced me," he said to Bill. "Be with you in a minute."

Bill drove fast, taking the shortcut through the creek so they could get a good parking place. He found a spot on the alley that ran along one side of the Hardware. Bill and Irv left to pick up some sodas. Isobel and Jeanne struck off down the cross alley toward the Presbyterian Church. Charlie turned sideways on the seat to see as much of what was happening up on Main Street as his alley view allowed.

Dusk tinged, then almost obscured the figures scuttling to get settled before the main event. Car hoods and fenders got loaded up. Then, as night deepened the street lights grew brighter, the drone of the announcers changed to an urgent rattle, speeding to get in every breathless detail as the background hubbub from the ring crowd rose to a steady roar. Down the dark side streets, the flare of a match or a cigarette brightening from a deep pull showed where listeners waited in autos and trucks.

When Izzy and Jeanne approached the side door to the church auditorium where C.E. was held a slim young man stepped under the light on the small stoop to identify himself.

"Oh, Kenny," Izzy said. Jeanne turned to look at her because she sounded sort of strange.

"Hello, Isobel" he said, "I thought you might like to walk around and see the sports crowd on its big night." He smiled at Jeanne to include her. Jeanne hadn't ever seen him before, but she guessed from his manners he'd come from a long ways away.

"Jeannie, this is Ken." Izzy's voice still sounded a little funny to Jeanne. "He's going to work at Staehli's shed this summer. Mr. Staehli knows his father."

Jeanne smiled back at him. She figured if he knew what time to meet Isobel at C.E. he must have done it before. Well, if Izzy was going out with a fruit tramp, she picked a good looking one. Ken had an air that reminded her of her brother Bill's, as though he knew he was safe from anyone being better than him, only not so bossy as Bill, more sort of graceful, instead. Kenny looked swell. She didn't see why Izzy wouldn't have told her about him. She'd talked about the ride she'd gone on accidentally with the new bank manager's son one night when somebody else from C.E. had driven them both home. He had sat with his cheek pressed hard to hers the whole way as though he was afraid otherwise he would have to say something. Isobel hadn't liked it. You could see she liked Ken by how shy she was now.

Izzy sounded worried when she answered him, "I can't, Kenny, Papa wouldn't like it."

"Your Dad isn't going anywhere outside the Nash, tonight, Izzy, Jeanne reminded her. Kenny shook her hand for that. Izzy looked scared and doubtful at the same time she was smiling. "You go ahead if you want, but Bill or Irv would spot me a block away," Jeanne added, "then they'd notice it was you with me. I better go on in now, and you come later."

Between rounds, when Frank Robison lowered the radio's blatting so people could hear themselves talk, hymns and hallelujahs drifted over from the bandstand down Main Street where the evangelists were raising Cain. Bill and Irv went to take a look at them, and came back to tell Charlie how funny they were, sputtering out mouthfuls of tiny lake flies that swarmed to the platform lights.

"Praise God," one of them had got out as he coughed, "if it wasn't for the lake flies we wouldn't appreciate it when they're gone." Somebody yelled, "The same goes for the preachers," but it sounded good natured, and nobody picked up on it. Every weekend, the street was crowded around the bandstand, and always a certain number of sinners would bow their heads and pray for salvation but tonight the fight drew most of the crowd

When Bill met Frank Hafner strolling with a German friend of his on Main Street, and mentioned Charlie was confined to the Nash with a bad back, the two hurried over to the alley with a couple of bottles of his home brewed beer. "Maybe it won't fix your back, but it sure won't do your mood any harm," he said. The friend laughed loudly and they sauntered off again, the friend's white painter's overalls showing faintly in the alley's dimness after Frank had been swallowed by it.

Charlie was just opening a bottle for himself when Gloria appeared, and ducked her head in through the car window. "Isn't one of those for me?" she asked. Charlie extended the other bottle out to her with the bruskness of exasperation. It looked like an attempt to be funny, but actually, it just about expressed the way he felt, which was that two beers were better than one.

Gloria had scandalized the town when she ran off and married Giorgio at the end of pear season, a few years before. It didn't matter if he did make a lot of money, people said, he was still nothing but a fruit tramp. As they showed up back in Lake County together to work the following years, Gloria was halfway slighted, and Giorgio was halfway accepted. Their status in Lake County never seemed to concern them.

Gloria got into the front seat beside Charlie with her beer, and sat with her legs tucked under her to the side. She twisted gracefully to slam the car door, and then took a swallow of beer, watching Charlie, as she tilted her head back. "Umm, good," she murmured.

"I didn't know you were a fights fan." Charlie said. "Where'd you leave Giorgio?"

"I came in to get cigarettes, silly. Giorgio doesn't like to come to town much." She lit a cigarette, and settled in serenely, as though the meeting had been arranged. "Why were you so sulky at the shed this morning?"

"Sulky! I felt like I'd been knocked down and tied up in a knot, and you looked amused. Besides, I never do enjoy having Giorgio lord it over me."

"He doesn't mean to," Gloria said. "He's just thinking about his boxes." Charlie sat up preternaturally straight and mimicked Giorgio spitting nails out and finically hammering them into an imaginary box. Gloria joined in, counting "seexty-seex, seexty-seven-." It was natural as walking to clown with Gloria. They had teamed up at it when she was a skinny little tomboy with a crush on the school's football hero. He invented gags, sometimes very elaborate ones and Gloria would get into the act. One winter they worked for days fabricating and burying what would look like a dead body from the school windows as one of Lake County's freak snowfalls melted away from it. One of her gags was to ask, regularly, "When are you going to take me out, Charlie?" He would regard her judiciously and say, "Next year, maybe."

When Isobel and Jeanne came back to the car later licking ice cream cones, Charlie leaned across Gloria abruptly opening the door on her side. "I wouldn't want to keep you," he said. She gave him a sidewise dirty look through lowered lashes, and laughed at him as she got out.

Charlie was careful to be cheerful when Bill dropped him and Isobel off after the evening. Trying to hide that he was more stiff and sore than ever made his walk painfully jaunty, like an old man's. Viv wanted to know who won the fight, and who had been in town. He relayed greetings to her and described how Walter Burns had arrived later than most of the crowd, driven by Mrs. Rawleigh in her cream Chrysler and how pleased with himself Walter seemed, like a bantam rooster with a big beautiful hen.

He amended his effective age from eighty to ninety as he struggled to open the slightly sticking door to the bedroom. He rocked himself over into bed and slowly straightened out his back, grunting with relief. "Here let me give you a rubdown," Viv said. She knelt over him, working seriously, putting her weight into it, thumping and kneading each arm and leg until she could feel the tension let go, and then finishing with long strokes down his back. Viv watched him anxiously.

"Is that better?" she asked. Amusement spread slowly over his face.

"Well, not really," he said, "but thanks anyway."

Viv laughed.

Chapter 3

Beulah liked to be up first in the morning, while the light came red and level through the scrub oaks. She shook down the ashes and scraped the grate so hard her flannel wrapper jounced around the top of her boots. It got her blood going. Sometimes Pa said it rattled him right out of bed when Beulah gave the grate a going-over.

While she filled the kettle at the sink she watched Gyp through the window. He came out of his dog house, stretching one back leg then the other out behind him till the muscles quivered. He shook himself then, businesslike, and started on his morning rounds, sniffing thoroughly before he lifted his leg to shoot exact jets onto certain rocks and bushes. The jingle of his collar got fainter as he wandered down the hill to the woodpile. He always stopped to check it for chipmunks or for the snake, but he didn't dwell on it this time. Beulah was glad he wasn't going to get overwrought about the snake this morning. Sometimes he would dig furiously at the smooth hole that slid under the neat-stacked wood sending showers of earth up behind him, yipping and snuffling excitedly for the scent, then snorting like a horse to get the dirt out of his nose. He would stand on his hind legs to claw at the wood, even try to pull chunks out of the stack with his teeth. Mr. Scott who camped in a tent close to the wood stack bawled Gyp out good when he did that. He had a right to, because he was the one who made wood out of the mush oaks Pa wanted cleared and corded it up so nice. His tent had square sides and a peaked roof, like a house. Early mornings when it was chilly she could see the glow from his little coal oil heater sprawled out like a big daisy on the canvas roof. It made her feel warm and safe to see that, the same as she felt when she rode with him to get their vegetables at Kate's stand. He drove steady and even, and he never forgot and left her there, either.

She thought she knew what bothered Gyp so much about the wood pile. It was seeing the snake's body going by in two opposite directions at the same time through spaces in the wood stack. She couldn't understand that herself but she liked to watch it. Pa said Gyp was fanatical about the snake; it didn't do any harm beyond stealing a few hens' eggs, and it kept down the vermin in the barn. Finally Gyp trotted out of sight into the dry gully. She stood wondering where he was going so briskly before breakfast like that, her mouth open a little, her light blue eyes rapt while the water spilled over the top of the kettle.

Pa had taught her how to build a good fire—don't strike any matches till after she poured the coal oil and wait till the flames started roaring up the chimney before setting the damper. She could follow Pa right along after he told her a few times over, as though his voice was still telling her, slow and even. He never got cross, as long as she was trying, except once in a while when everything started to go wrong at once, then he would holler "Beulah, you fool!" and come hobbling to set things right. It was only natural for a person to get flustered sometimes.

After she got dressed and had the eggs jiggling in the boiling water, the mush puffing out slow steam signals and the coffee just beginning to smell rich, she called the men to come eat. Some people thought she was dumb, she knew that, but if she had a chance to put her whole mind to it, she could get breakfast just as well as anybody, and she was proud of it.

Her father and Ernie, the hired man, came up the hill from the turkey corral, Colson moving with a bent-over, gliding lurch. Years ago Daniel Colson had turned his new Fordson tractor over on himself, and his broken back had mended crookedly. His tractor had been the first one in the county. Some people thought the accident had been a judgment on him for bringing the noisy, smelly contraption into the valley, and for his free thinking in general. Also, they said, he had no business not going back to the hospital for his treatments, like he was supposed to. It was as though he stayed crippled on purpose. Panting slightly by the time he reached the house, Colson propped himself against the door frame to rest a minute before he spoke.

"The turkey under the manzanita has left the nest again," he told his daughter. He tipped his head back along his bent backbone to survey the collection of hutches in the corral with fatalistic serenity.

Holding the boiled eggs under the cold tap for a second, Beulah remembered how hot the glass nest egg had felt when the reached under the Rhode Island Red to get the eggs for breakfast.

"Pa," she said, after consideration, "I think the red hen is getting broody." She told him how the chicken had turned her head around to glare at her and pecked her arm twice, but had stuck to the nest instead of going off in a huff, the way she ordinarily would.

"Why, I'll bet you're right, Beulah," her father said. "I hope so. It would be the best solution possible if Red took over the turkey nest."

"That's right," Ernie agreed. Beulah glowed at all the praise.

They settled at the table and ate in gratified silence until they heard Gyp release a burst of scolding barks down by the barn.

Colson was expecting Jess Sooter who owned the ranch to the north to come in during the morning to talk about hiring a spray rig for both their places, but Gyp wouldn't bark like that at Jess. Ernie went to the window. "Who is it, Ernie?" Colson asked. A stranger was coming up the hill, Ernie reported. Colson went to stand in the doorway. The intruder approached with deliberate steps, head down, watching his own feet. He was a narrow-built man with a long oblong face, sandy hair parted in the middle, a wide straight-lipped mouth and eyes the color of muscats. He wore a black suit-coat over bib overalls, and held a black hat before him in his hands.

"Mr. Colson?" he asked.

"Yes."

"I'm Reverend Harper, Elliott Harper." He offered his hand, and Colson shook it once. "You've probably heard about the revival we are holding in town. I'd appreciate a word with you, especially about the little lady here." He nodded his head toward Beulah, standing raw-boned and tall as himself, gazing at him, her lower lip hanging soft with wonder. Visitors to the ranch were usually just the druggist, Mr. Douglas, who was Pa's chess partner, or the newcomer, Mr. Winton. Them or the Watkins Man. Sometimes when Mr. Winton came over and talked late, they laughed so hard it woke her up. This new man looked like it would hurt him to smile, let alone laugh. Nobody had ever come to see Pa about her before.

"May I come in?" the Reverend urged politely.

Colson let him enter, but remained standing. He turned to Beulah, "I tell you what you better do now, Beulah," he said. "Go down and see if you can get the red hen to take the turkey nest and stay with her till she settles in." Reluctant as she was to miss what the stranger had to say, Beulah started off without question, glad Pa had given her such a responsible job while the new man could hear. She pulled her jacket on as she went. It was an old coat of her father's twenty years out of date, warm and easy on her shoulders when she worked. A heavy twill skirt protected her bare legs down to her cracked boots, and a man's black felt hat, worn undented, covered her hair.

"Now, what is it you want?" Colson said to the preacher.

"I've come to ask you to come in to the meeting and bring your daughter with you, Mr. Colson. Give her a chance to get in touch with the Lord, which it seems she hasn't had."

"No," Colson said, mildly. "No, we won't be doing that."

The preacher regarded him steadily with candid green eyes. "I've got to tell you, Mr. Colson, people in town don't think you're doing the right thing to keep a big girl like her shut up here all the time, doing your farm work for you, and dressed almost like a man. They think she ought to see other folks more, other women, so she can get some idea of what a woman ought to be like."

Colson doubled over even farther than usual, with exasperation. "Mr. Harper," he declared, "the last thing in the world Beulah needs is to be thinking what she ought to be like and isn't. It's plain to see that if the Lord made Beulah, he botched the job, but she does well with what was dealt her. She has a loving disposition, and she likes to work. That's her salvation right there."

The preacher stood listening his eyes learning the linoleum pattern. He looked up. "You've got to think of her immortal soul, though," he said, "and you've no right to keep her benighted."

Colson suppressed a retort to that. "Think of it this way, Mr. Harper, just for your peace of mind." His voice was patient. "If Beulah there had been born smart, I'd have made an atheist out of her by the time she was twelve, couldn't have helped myself, so according to you she'd have been headed straight for hell. As it is she's as innocent as the day she issued from the hand of the Lord, so you're ahead of the game already."

They had been standing all the while they were talking, and Colson was shaking a little now, from anger or fatigue, and nearly stumbled as he turned. The preacher caught his arm quickly and supported him. "Now, is that all?" Colson asked coldly, drawing away.

"Well, no. Remember you've got an itinerant living down there," he indicated the flat below with a sidewise jerk of his head. "People say that's just asking for trouble with a girl like Beulah."

Colson backed up till he could lean against the wall, and stood a while breathing hard with his head lowered, like somebody either praying for patience or gathering his forces for a charge. Finally he said, "Ernie, please take this man to the gate and let him out."

Harper bowed to Beulah as they passed her beside the turkey nest with the glistening big red chicken on it. Beulah didn't feel as easy with the chicken as she would have it if had been a turkey. Once she had overheard her father tell Mr. Douglas while they were playing chess, "Beulah may be a simpleton but she's the best hand with turkeys I ever had." That gave her a lot of confidence with the turkeys. They were delicate. When one came down with a roupy look and swollen glands from a draft or wet footing she would wrap its head in a sock and coax its appetite with grasshoppers she caught under an M.J.B. can. Usually it would look mollified and recover. Turkeys were good company, at least the babies and hens were. Gobblers were bossy and standoffish. She had watched them by the hour when she was young, awed by the great fan they could make of their tails, the mysterious rumble from their puffed-out chests and the bronze-colored light shaking from their feathers. Their stiff downstretched wing tips would score circles in the dust as they strutted around a quiet hen picking at bugs or dusting her feathers. Most of the time the hens would scurry off and start scratching for food a ways off, but sometimes one would stay, squatting in the dust as the big gobbler mounted her back to tread her until at some mysterious signal she would flip up her tail just at the moment his bent down and they joined. Beulah would watch, leaning against the crossbar gate, transfixed with thrill.

The turkey corral on the slope was dotted with wooden huts thatched with brush to protect the fowls from the hot summers and give them privacy. It looked like a tiny village. The flat that spread out below it, with the barn in its center, was edged by a twisting barranca, sharply cut into the clay by run-off from the hills. Beulah watched the preacher's car ease out of sight into its deep gully and crawl up the other side. She watched the flivver bounce along the road, mid-height between the dry yellow corn, and the orchard's dark green. The barranca twisted off to the left, and you could keep track of it by the clumps of bushes along the bank, and an occasional big oak Pa had left stand right at the edge of the field, though the corn grew thin and poor close to it. Not a leaf was stirring this morning, but when the wind was up you could hear the big leaves of the corn clashing like sharpening knives. She never went into the corn field except to pick a little sweet corn for the table. It was the place she liked the least. When you hurried between the rows, the leaves scratched and prickled, almost as though they lashed out at you.

The main road ran along the front of their place, with Kelsey Creek just a little beyond. It flowed peacefully now, but in a bad winter storm it could toss over its banks and swirl in a brown, frothing flood with whole trees tossing in it, twenty times its regular width. The water went down quick when the rain stopped, but it left a queer good-for-nothing dry bed of silty, bare sand between the stones and boulders, and a level line where dirty tangles of twigs and grass caught far up in the trees and bushes showed how high it had been. Beulah thought it looked scary, and wished it was pretty on the other side of the creek like it was on theirs, but Pa said it was a good thing the water had some place to rampage in when it went wild, otherwise it would tear at the soil and wash it away. That waste land was what kept the ranch safe. The chicken shuffled its legs, quietly settling down, and Beulah dozed off.

When she woke up the hen was still sitting stiffly on the eggs, looking straight ahead.

It seemed to Beulah the preacher had no more than got out of sight when another car showed up on the road. All this coming and going confused her, till she recognized from the round shape of his head and the brown hair fitted like a cap smooth as silk to it, that it was Jess. Jess usually just walked down from his place next door when he came to see Pa, instead of driving in like that.

Chapter 4

About the first thing Beulah could remember was the day the stile was finished and Pa taught her and Jess to get over it. Jess and Beulah had been friends since they were babies. When they were big enough to visit, Colson, seeing neither one was clever enough to manage the gate latch, built a stile between the two ranches for them to climb over. He tried to teach them to turn around and go down backwards, once they got to the top, but they had giggled and gone thumping down the steps on their behinds, over and over till they were sore. Beulah remembered the breezy day, and blossoms drifting down, and there was something else she could almost see that stayed just under her memory, like a fish dimpling the water from below, something under the pear tree, pretty and bright, like a big bouquet. She would get the beauty-feeling of it, but he could never quite see it.

Almost every day she and Jess would scramble over the stile to meet for games or to splash in the shallow swimming hole in the creek. Soon a clear-worn path focused at the stile from both sides. As the years passed, and they had both been taken up with the hard work of the farms, the path was grown over with weeds and grass, and gradually disappeared.

Last year, in the spring, Beulah had taken the first hatch of poults on an outing to forage in the overgrown home orchard by the stile. It was as hot as a full summer's day. The turkeys sat nodding and jerking awake again like old men, chirping every once in a while, as though they had just remembered something. When she got too hot, she had climbed over the stile to go down to the swimming hole where Jess and she used to swim. She laughed because it only came to her waist now, where in those days she felt very strong and brave when she had swum across the deepest part. Now she could hardly let out for a few strokes before she was across it. She had gotten dressed and seated herself beneath the gnarled pear tree with her skirt spread wide between her knees to make a nest for the little turkeys to hop in and out of the way they liked to do, when Jess came over to the fence to speak to her.

"I wasn't going to let on I watched you, Beulah," Jess said, "but you looked so pearly and nice in the water, I thought I would tell you." Beulah beamed serenely across her lapful of poults, showing them off as proudly as a hen. Jess's gaze followed up the arrow her thighs made. He climbed over the stile and stood looking down at her, his hat politely in his hand, then sank on an elbow beside her on the grassy rise in his stiff overalls and rubber boots and reached with deference toward the dark patch where the thighs met. She leaned back on her elbows watching him with wonderment while the poults spilled to the ground peeping in protest.

Beulah didn't look cross, like the whore Muriel did when she sometimes let him in, up against a tree during intermission at the dance at the I.O. of O.F. hall when it was rainy and her business wasn't good. She didn't hurry him, either, but reached out and touched the shaved line of his hair on his neck. He got to his feet, hauling at the straps of his overalls, hopping on one foot as he pulled them off. Beulah sat up, then rolled over onto her knees and planted her hands in the grass. Jess raised his face with a look of fierce thanksgiving as he pushed home.

Though the paths that met at the stile were gradually wearing clear again, Jess didn't come to the house much, except like now when he and Pa were figuring on sharing extra hired hands for the fruit season. They usually went in together for any work they had to hire done in their adjoining orchards. Colson did the planning and made the arrangements, and Jess pitched in with any hard labor needed. Jess liked to help Pa with the heavy jobs, or the touchy ones like patching the barn roof, but he didn't like to telephone. He said he couldn't do like Pa and talk to somebody on the phone as though he was right there when he wasn't.

Beulah wished she could get back to the house to see Jess, but she didn't want to lose out with the hen after getting this far. She stayed by it until lunch time. It ate a lot of the mash she had brought it and began to blink slowly and doze a little, like it had finally settled in.

She felt full of satisfaction as she climbed the hill, and started to get the things out for lunch. Colson watched her as she moved about the kitchen. "You're getting fat, Beulah," he observed as she served him.

"No, I'm not, Pa. Only here." She spread her arms. "I'm going to have a baby."

"How's that," Colson asked mildly.

"Jess comes over the stile," she explained. Colson went on eating his cold pork roast and potato salad. He thought back to the day he had finished the stile, how Beulah and Jess had giggled and shrieked, and how long it had taken them to master climbing over it. He also remembered Beulah's mother under the pear tree in a pink dress, so delicate she seemed to float with the wind. She had watched the three of them without a word, her head sinking lower and lower as she watched till she was holding it up with her hands covering her eyes. She had come to stand in front of him finally, still with her head down, and said, "Daniel, there no use for me to try. I can't stand this. I'm going back to Baltimore and try to forget I ever saw either one of you." She had raised her face then, her clear eyes so wide open it seemed to Colson he could see right through her head. She turned and started away through a drift of blossoms, holding her wide hat on when it slipped with a raised arm as though she were hurrying through a pelting storm. Colson had limped after her, almost blind with dismay and confusion until suddenly he saw, clearly as an outsider, what an absurd figure he must cut, how grotesque his crippled body and the hapless children on the stile must seem to his dainty young wife. He gave up the pursuit and stood a long time staring down until he got calmed down enough that his heart wouldn't burst, telling himself, "Minnie's nature is fitted only for a smooth course. She's done pretty well, considering." He had straightened himself stiffly, and stared at the sky dry-eyed until they smarted.

Beulah brought him his peach pie. "Well, I tell you what you better do, Beulah," he said. "Best thing probably is for you and Jess to get married. Jess can move in here, and Ernie can move on over to Jess's place to keep an eye on it—I don't think Ernie would object to that."

He considered Beulah standing before him shedding a kind of goofy radiance. He should have known better than to expect her to just go on mothering poults all her life. By sheer chance that confounded preacher had turned out to be right—Beulah would have to go among the women, now. She would need them to steer her through.

"Why don't you get yourself some dresses and a lady's coat when you go in to town Thursday, Beulah," he said. "Get some shoes, too."

He scanned the future, laying quick plans against whatever chance might bring. Chance. He mustn't underestimate that powerful lady. He straightened up as far as his back would let him. Here he was getting set for misfortune when, actually, except for Beulah and Jess, both family lines were perfectly sound. The odds weren't the best, but still there was a chance they might get a child with more brains than the two of them put together.

Chapter 5

Beth came into the Hafners' kitchen from the spare bedroom where she had a beauty parlor fixed up so she could give finger waves and marcels to get herself some spending money. Now she was out of school, Pa wouldn't give her any. She carried curling tongs in her hand.

"That sure was the funniest marcel I ever gave anybody," she said. "There wasn't hardly anything for the tongs to get hold of, only wisps and straggles." She lifted graceful fingers where Beulah's imagined hair was spread out. "She said she wanted it nice because she's going to get married soon. I curled and back-combed it till every hair was doing double duty, but it still looked like she had little brown dust mice on her head instead of hair." She lifted a lock of her own hair back from her temple. It fell rich and dark against the ivory of her cheek.

Her mother stood before the big iron kitchen range, the bow of her apron ties nodding above the expanse of her hips as she stirred her ravioli sauce. Beth's stomach tightened as she noticed Bill Winton's kid sister in the pantry buttering a slice of bread that had just come out of the oven, judging by the smell in the kitchen.

"Oh, hi, Jeanne," Beth said lightly. You never knew what that stringy little kid would carry back to Bill, and the worst part was Bill took her seriously.

Jeanne's green eyes were non-committal over the big bite of bread she was taking. "Hi," she said.

Beth's story tapered off. "She's sure the homeliest bride I ever worked on."

Liz eyed her daughter neutrally. "Maybe so," she said, tasting a spoonful of sauce for thickness, "but together her and Jess's places will make the best ranch on Kelsey Creek."

The shining points of Beth's King Tut hairdo sickled across her cheeks as she tossed her head to signal Ma to lay off her. She was two years out of high school and still not married, and according to Ma's timetable, scheduled to lose her looks before she was twenty-five, like women did in the old country. She smoothed her hands down her slim waist and flaring hips. As if she would ever let herself get round as a barrel the way Ma was. "Herb says they call Jess 'one-ball Reilly' down at the pool-hall," she giggled.

Liz raised her eyebrows and wobbled her head almost rakishly. She had seen the dazzled, peaceful look of pregnancy on Beulah's face when she let her into Babe's beauty parlor. That look was the first thing that showed on a woman who liked being pregnant, even before her breasts started to plump up. Beth watched her mother, fascinated. "What?" she asked, as though Liz had actually spoken. "You're kidding." She thought it funny that with her looks and figure she should have to feel jealous of a camel-faced dim-wit like Beulah. Her own future was still over the horizon with not a thing in sight, unless you counted Earl, who couldn't support hisself let alone a wife.

Pa didn't mind letting her know he felt she was a burden either, lately. "I'll feed you, all right," he said, "but I can't carry you for all that drugstore stuff you get, lip rouge, and 'Gauzettes,' and a new pair of silk stockings every time you turn around."

She went back into her bedroom so Bill's sister wouldn't see how mad she was, and flumped down on her bed with a copy of Screen Stories opened to "Lilac Time" on her knees. Ma seemed sure Beulah was pregnant already, too. If she was, that was one thing she didn't envy her.

Instead of reading, she watched the window curtain breathing into the room over her bed and then getting sucked flat against the screen as the erratic afternoon wind started and failed. A long ripple curled the ruffled edge as the curtain bellied inward again. She raised her arm to let it coast along her skin and shivered.

She wondered if Bill was going to ask her to the dance at Lakeport this Saturday. That would make four County dances all told if he did. Already people would ask her, "Where's Bill?" or "Is Bill coming?" as if she was his girl. She the closest thing to it he had. Nobody had any strings on Bill—you could tell that by the way he acted. Pleasant and nice, but taking off whenever he wanted, so nobody could expect anything. She wanted to be Bill's girl so much it scared her.

She smiled, remembering the first time she ever saw him, last year, at a party where everybody came, all ages. She'd been back in the kitchen with Ma and when she returned to the living room, Pa was singing Pagliacci as usual when he was feeling good at a party. He was straining on the high notes, arms out wide, notes like Caruso on the record, holding his arms out wide and almost sobbing while Wint played a beautiful accompaniment and Bill strummed along on a banjo-uke. Wint's back was very straight, but not stiff looking as he played. His coal black hair had curled up into ringlets on his head with the heat, but his profile looked dignified and commanding. He never looked fine like that when she saw him working outside, away from the piano. Wint was the one person who seemed more natural dressed up than when he was in work clothes. Though he didn't look like Wint, much—Bill was taller and his dark hair was a dark brown, where Wint's was jet black but the main difference was his nose had a wave in it instead of being aquiline like his father's—she had figured right away that the boy with the banjo was Wint's son Bill, home from college. Bill's head was bent over so he could see the frets and his lower lip was caught under his eyetooth on the right side while he got his fingers in place. When he got set right for a chord he would let loose the lip and look up with a big smile. Then when the chord would changes Wint would look over at him struggling again and say "b flat" or "dominant," as he played along perfectly, and Bill would start hunting again. She loved the sight of that tooth denting his brownish-pink lip. She got to know later it meant he was thinking harder than usual even, and then it made her uneasy. She was afraid of what Bill might think of her, somehow.

When they applauded Pa's Caruso act, Bill raised his round arched eyebrows and half bowed too. You could see he was spoofing himself, but you couldn't be sure whether he was laughing at Pa's performance, too. Not at his own father's, though, because Wint was really a musician. He could play anything you named, right off. It seemed a wonder he hadn't had a job playing piano, he was so good.

Later when Wint was playing 'Dardinella' Bill couldn't keep up with the chord changes at all. He put the banjo-uke down on his chair and asked her to dance, and later after she helped Ma serve the refreshments, he came over to eat with her.

He didn't even ask what her name was before he started up sort of a game, talking about the other people in the room as if they were history characters. Pa was the Kaiser, and Wint was Showpan. Lacy Smith's kid, Emerson, who had been asleep in the bedroom but woke up for the food, he called Homer.

Then she had thought up calling Lacy Smith and his wife Lord and Lady Lacy, which made her laugh because of the sound, and because they were the poorest of the whole bunch. From Kentucky. Their house was just a shack with a Congoleum rug in the front room with nothing under it but bare earth. She'd never seen anything like it. Bill's game wasn't too mean, though, because everybody got to be grander than they really were, but the way he hit the nail on the head about people he saw for the first time was scary. She started to worry about what he would think of her and that made her mad, because she knew what she thought of him, already. She wanted him, period.

Bill asked who she wanted to be, and she said, Cleopatra, who she read about when they dug up King Tut. She was glad she knew that much history at least. When she asked Bill who he wanted to be, he looked totally surprised, and said he would have to think about that one.

For all he talked, Bill never talked about himself or about her, and especially not about them, Beth noted unhappily. She never knew anyone like that before. She didn't know why she liked Bill so much, but she did. When she walked into a dance hall with him, she felt like she was dressed in diamonds and could wrap the other girl's envy around her like silk.

Suddenly it occurred to her that Jeanne was hanging around because she expected Bill to pick her up on his way home from work. She swung off the bed and hauled on her black wool bathing suit fast then strolled back into the kitchen.

"You going back down to the creek again?" she asked Jeanne casually. "I'll go down with you if you want."

They went single file through a mowed hay field along a path of silvery trampled straw narrow as an animal trail. The sun was hot on their backs, though it was far enough down to cast long shadows ahead of them as they walked. At the bottom of the sloping field the creek ran, edged with trees and bushes, wild roses, willow, and bay trees whose exposed roots gleamed like pewter where swimmers had climbed over them year after year. On the far side a patch of fine gray sand tilted toward the water, backed by tall flickering cottonwoods with curtains of wild grape hanging from them, and guarded by deep blackberry thicket. A narrow path led in from the road. Upstream, bay trees clustered to spread dark shade on the stones and gravel and the water ran shallow except for a single channel through the boulders.

Beth eased herself into the water at a shallow place and swam across the creek with graceful arm strokes holding her head up stiffly to keep her hair dry. She settled on the sunniest of the sand patches, wriggling into its warmth, and buried her head in her folded arms to steep in daydreams. She imagined Bill beside her, talking, as usual, and turning occasionally to look at her with his bright hazel eyes, checking her on something he was saying. His arm was around her and his hand stroked her shoulder absently, holding it hard and then letting up, then pressing again, as he did sometimes as he talked. She thought Bill must know the way that made her feel, but usually he didn't stop talking. His thoughts always seemed to be away, about a different time and place, but at least so far they weren't about a different girl.

She burrowed deeper into the warm sand. If Bill would take her away with him, maybe she could amount to something herself more than just another Lake County housewife tying her apron strings in a bow over her behind as it spread. She dreamed how pretty she would look even in an apron getting dinner ready for Bill in an apartment in San Francisco. The dream-doorbell rang and she went to let Bill in. She could see her own face looking radiant as she swung the door open. A stranger was standing there and she could see how his face lit up with a look of admiration when he saw her. He was from L.A., he said, and in the movie business, looking for a friend who used to live in their apartment. Then he excused himself for staring at her, but he couldn't help it and said she was a natural and should come see him about a screen test. He murmured something about Hedy Lamarr, who everybody said she looked like, and was writing something down for her on his card when Bill came home. Bill could see he had a pretty extraordinary wife after all and the movie agent could see right away what a smart husband she had. The sand caked quickly along Beth's wet sides in the dry air and she snored softly into her pillowing arms.

Jeanne thought it would be a good time to get a bottle of beer for Bill up from the creek bottom, while nobody was around to learn about the secret cache. The Hafners had hidden gunny sacks full of their homemade wine and beer in the creek when they got tipped off in the spring that prohibition agents were going to raid the Rincon. Some bottles had fallen out of the sacks when they tried to retrieve them later, and were still there, half silted over. The secret cache of beer was her and Bill's secret. She swam downstream watching the bank for her landmark, an old willow tree hanging over the place where the water was darkest and deepest. She blew out most of her breath and turned under in a duck dive to forage among the mossy rough stones looming dimly on the bottom for as long as her breath held out, then she fought her way up to the circle of light glimmering like a tin lid above her. She gulped a few breaths of air at the surface then turned under to hunt again. She had just spotted the curve of a bottle among the stones when a tremor in the water made her look up almost nose to nose with a big glaring face rimed with tiny air bubbles on the mustache and eyebrows. She scrambled past a body that seemed big as a walrus, but immediately the big intruder surged past her as she struggled back up the watery light well and was watching with a stern expression when she finally surfaced, panting with exhaustion. When she got over being frightened by the seeming monster, she was scared he was some kind of prohibition officer that had heard about the beer in the creek, and she was in trouble. Nobody else who knew about the sunken beer could find it; it was practically hers and Bill's and now the secret was spoiled. She started to protest, but sank and bobbed up choking and spluttering.

"Sorry I scared you. If you'll just relax, I'll give you a tow," the walrus said. He gathered her hair gently in his hand and towed her back upstream to the landing place. It was smooth as riding in a canoe.

"That's a good way to tow somebody," Jeanne granted when she could sit up in the shallows. "Thanks."

"You let your breath out before you dive, don't you," the stranger said.

"It's all right," she assured him. "I have to. I can't get down to the bottom otherwise."

He shook his head, and said with flat authority, "It's not safe. It's possible that sometime you might not make it back to the surface. Do you know that? What are you looking for anyway?"

"Just some bottles of beer."

"Really. At least, you ought to have somebody watching you." Jeanne listened. Remembering how expertly he had towed her, she thought he might know what he was talking about.

"I'll just go down when my brother is here, then," she conceded, "but please don't tell anybody. It would be gone in no time."

"I won't even take any myself. You're a good swimmer. How how old are you?"

"Almost thirteen." She knew what would be next. "Little for your age, aren't you?"

"'Immature' is what they usually say." The stranger smiled so broadly his teeth showed beneath his stiff red mustache. A mat of fine red-gold hair spread over his shoulders and chest. The hair on his head was darker, more auburn. He had a deep chest and more muscles than anybody she had ever seen. She didn't want him to say the same things other people said about her.

He only said, "You'll get over that," and turned over to lie face down among the weedy pebbles. A terrible knotted scar slashed across his back. Jeanne stared at the cruel twists and gouges.

"How'd you get that?" she asked.

"Logging," he said, not fully raising his chin from his crossed wrists. "Cable snapped with a load of logs on it."

"I'm sorry," Jeanne's voice sounded pinched. It was about the worst thing she had ever seen.

"I was lucky, I just got a flick of the end. It could have cut me in two."

Jeanne touched the small round puckers around a deep gouged hole wonderingly. "What made it this way?"

"Drains. It got my lung a little."

Over on her sunny bank, Beth raised her eyelids and stirred. She propped up on an elbow and craned her neck to see the whole empty stretch of the swimming hole. She jumped up to the edge, shading her eyes with one hand as she squinted in the direction of the leafy clumps hiding Jeanne and the logger.

"Jeanne," she called with a rising querulous tone.

"Yeah," Jeanne yelled back, and rose grudgingly to thread her way through the willow tangle to the open beach. The stranger followed her into the clearing and stood behind her looking over at Beth.

"Will you come over here," Beth called. It was a testy command, not a question. Jeanne shrugged and slid into the water from the soapstone bank.

"Bye," she called over her shoulder. Beth bent down at the opposite bank scolding her in a whisper before she even got out of the water.

"What ever were you doing off in the brush like that with a strange man?"

"Don't be so creepy," Jeanne snapped. "He just saved me from drowning."

"You couldn't drown if you wanted to." Beth said, her voice sounding new depths of exasperation.

"You don't know. He says I could."

Jeanne's sullen look changed to sudden gladness as she glanced beyond Beth's shoulder—that meant Bill had arrived. Beth turned with a radiant smile on her own face to watch as he lifted a trailing grapevine out of the way of a short, blond man with a bright pink sunburn. Bill looked dark as an Indian beside him. His face was caked with dust, and his hair was wet almost to dripping with sweat, but the way he smiled when he brought the new man over made him handsomer than ever. She would give a million dollars, she thought, to see Bill look that proud when he introduced her to somebody.

"Beth, this is Irv," he said. "I told you he might come up for a visit."

"Oh, I recognize you, Irv." Beth's smile widened to show a lot of her even teeth. "You're the strong man in Bill's 'living pyramid' photograph."

"That's me," Irv said. His smile began to spread to match Beth's. "Bottom of the stack."

"Maybe so," Beth said, "but I'd like to see any of the others hang up there by hisself without you under him."

Bill raised his head, noting her new staunch tone and straightforward smile with interest. They settled in the sunny spot, with Irv in the shade at the edge because of his sunburn. They made some jokes about his color, and talked about his visit, and the summer. Irv was elated at how easy they all thought it would be for him to get work.

"How come your boss would lay you off, when he used to say you were the one he could always count on," Jeanne asked indignantly.

"That was what Barney always said, but they laid him off too. They fired everybody who hadn't been there more than three years." He stared down at the ground. No matter what anybody could say about the times and conditions he was ashamed of losing his job.

When the shade from trees on the far bank began to reach them Bill said his bath was getting cold and made a running shallow dive from the edge of the beach. He swam under water a long way before he surfaced blowing and slinging his hair away from his face. Drops from it made a dotted circle around him where he stood waist deep. "Bring me the soap, will you, Umps?" he called.

Beth was propped on an elbow, facing Irv. "How come you've known Bill so long? Are you related?"

"No, but just about by now. We own the house next to theirs, and nobody ever thought of moving till Pod got sick."

"Oh, in Oakland," Beth nodded. "What's it like in Oakland? Like the City?" The "City" meant San Francisco.

Irv shook his head. "I'll say not."

They watched Jeanne get the soap from Bill's rolled up white towel and start swimming sidestroke toward the shallows with it held up dry in one hand.

Beth persisted. "Where was it you worked?"

"Amory Johnson's, a big, stationery outfit. I was in the mailing room but I was supposed to be working my way up."

"What were the girls like in the mail room. Were they pretty?"

Irv considered a minute. "Pretty enough, I guess."

"What about the rest. Aren't there any really pretty ones in the other offices?"

"Yeah, well, sure there are." He looked down, then up at her again with a look that was a tribute. Her skin was creamy ecru against her black hair and black bathing suit, her lipstick still crimson and perfect. There were pretty girls, but none anywhere near so pretty as Beth. He wanted to say that, yet it didn't seem that Beth was dwelling on the question just to get a compliment. Anybody that pretty must be sick of compliments by now.

"Have you got a girl in the company?"

"Not really. I'm mostly busy. I work nights, too, at the Country Club. Bell hop." He looked to see if that disappointed her.

"You do! Two jobs. Why do you do that?"

"Well, I'm what Mom calls the 'breadwinner' of the family since my old man died, but I don't 'win' much an hour, so I work nights, too."

"That doesn't sound fair." Beth seemed worked up. "Doesn't your brother work too?"

"He does now, for the summer, thank God. But he's got to start college in the fall."

"How come he has to and not you?"

"Oh, Ben's got to go to college. He's awfully smart, in school anyway."

"Like Bill," Beth said.

"Yes—" he drew it out, trying to figure what was the difference. "No, not like Bill. Ben is just good at school."

Beth nodded. Bill was smart any way you looked at it.

"Is it fun, working at the club? Are there women working there too?"

"Well, sure, they're around, but they're—older." Considering his opinion of the women help and guests at the country club, he thought 'older' was a pretty gentle word for it.

"You must think I'm awfully inquisitive but I wonder all the time what it would be like, working and living in the city."

"Not like Lake County, I can tell you that." Irv looked around with pleasure.

"Oh, Lake County," Beth registered disdain. Her gaze settled on Irv and she looked like she was on the edge of giggling as she watched him.

"What's the matter?"

"I'm not laughing at you; it's your sunburn. Bill should have told you to be careful about the sun up here. It's fierce. You look like the drawings I used to make in grammar school. My pink and yellow crayons always wore out first." Downstream, Jeanne joined Bill at the ford. She tossed him the soap and glanced back at the beach. "She was asking him to tell her about Oakland," Jeanne said. "You'd think that would be a stopper, wouldn't you?"

Bill looked down at her with amusement. "Don't be jealous, Umps." He caught his lip under a tooth and started to lather his arms. "Everything's going to be fine."

Irv still hadn't gotten into the water when Bill and Jeanne swam back to the beach. Bill said he had to go into town for a sack of chicken feed before he went home and would see them in a half hour or so up at Beth's house on his way back. Irv edged into the water. "I feel like my face would pop if I dove in," he said.

"We'll go up to the house as soon as you're done." Beth said. "I want to get some Unguentine on you."

"Umps," Irv called from the middle of the creek. "Where am I supposed to go for a bath?"

"Anywhere by the crossing," she answered. "Wait a second, I'll bring you the soap." The water felt silky, and glimmered in the shadows. When she was opposite Beth on the beach again, Jeanne hollered she was going to swim on to the mill, and would see them up at the house in a little while. The logger was just climbing out on the beach when she got back. "Goodbye Umps!" he called over his shoulder, smiling.

Jeanne bridled. "Where did you get that?"

"How could I help? It's what they holler when they want you. I gathered you liked it."

"Well, I guess I do," Jeanne said. "Anyway, you can call me whatever you like."

By the time Jeanne got back to the Hafner kitchen Beth was soothing salve on Irv's face with gentle fingers. He bent toward her touch the way a cat will lean in when you pet it.

Of all the things she had seen Beth do to get attention, Jeanne thought, this was the first time she had ever seen her just being nice.

Bill took the shortcut to town that stayed down in the bottomland close to the creek. The road, beneath the mesa, was shadowy and cool. He slouched along comfortably, enjoying the escape from the heat, and eased the Nash into the creek when they came to the crossing. By the end of summer the ford would dwindle to a shallow riffle, or to just a string of puddles along a dry channel of gray stones and boulders, but now in June, waves rippled along the running-board as the Nash strained and slid over the submerged rocks and shifting gravel like a foundering ox. Bill drove with his hands loose on the wheel to let the car accommodate to the bottom, watching the water for hazards, thinking about the summer ahead. Beth seemed easy with Irv—easier than she was with him, actually. The way she boosted Irv as hero of the living pyramid you'd think she was Irv's girl. He noted with interest the twinge of jealousy he felt. With Irv around he was reverting to the time when they were kids doing everything together, in Oakland. He hadn't thought about Oakland for months. Right now he'd better think about the future—or he wouldn't have one. He'd stayed here a year longer than he intended already. He hated to leave but much as he liked ranching, it was time he got going.

He stopped at the feed store, and then, with a gunny sack of wheat propped up on the seat like a companion, he drew up at the pay phone outside the hardware store and called his boss at the Oaks. Bill told him he wanted to see the division manager who was scheduled to come up from the City, Saturday, but the boss said he'd cancelled the Kelseyville visit. He was held up longer than he thought; he would be in Calistoga. Bill said, fine, he'd catch him in Calistoga, then.

"Sorry I won't be able to make the dance Saturday," he told Beth when he stopped to pick up Irv and Jeanne. "I have to go into Calistoga, and there isn't any bus back at night. You and Irv ought to go though."

It was close to dinner time when the three drove out the narrow driveway that ran to the road. While they were stopped at the gate, a light truck rattling along the main road turned abruptly into their lane and jerked to a stop, inches from the Nash.

The driver, a big young man whose straight hair and skin were both the color of a camel hair coat, let his hands drop from the wheel and sat looking at Bill, waiting. Frank Hafner was in the seat beside him.

"Back up and let them go home, Earl," Frank said wearily.

Earl gunned the truck into a backward arc, and again, dropped his hands to wait.

Bill waved acknowledgment to Frank and headed home. "What was that about?" Irv asked.

"Beats me," Bill said. "That was Frank Hafner, but it wasn't his truck. I don't know who the driver was."

"That was Earl Green," Jeanne said. "He and Frank drive out to a job out at the Springs together."

"But why all the drama?" Irv asked.

"I think he was just acting smart," Jeanne said.

Chapter 6

In the gray early light Irv lay flat on his back on his cot mattress with his eyes closed tight, his forehead clenched with worry and the sheet caught between his teeth. Bill, dressed except for his shoes, stood looking down at him, his expression mirroring Irv's.

"All out," he said. "Execution is at 7:30."

Irv turned his head and regarded him with what would have been a wan look, except for his glowing sunburn, and the intense blue it made his eyes. "If it's so funny, you tell me why an orchard boss would want to hire a mail room clerk."

"Your past will remain a secret with me." Bill tried to lift one side of the cot to dump Irv out of it. "Don't worry, they'll hire you, but you have to get up first." He reached across Irv and began rolling him to the edge. Irv suffered this for one revolution, then hooked an arm around Bill's neck and swiftly pinned him flat to the cot. As they struggled, one of its legs began to fold. Irv got clear and threw Bill to the braided rug between their beds, where he lay still in a twisted posture of death, one arm flung across his face.

When Irv was dressed, he nudged Bill with his foot. "Let's go," he said. "I smell breakfast."

"Ah, yes. Your last."

They came downstairs, their footsteps slurred and syncopated in long ago perfected patterns. They built top-heavy towers of the pancakes, bacon and eggs Mrs. Winton had ready for them. "You'd think you were still ten," she said. She stood at the tall blue enameled range flipping more cakes. The light above the kitchen table was lit, and the windows had steamed up so they looked bright even though it was still dim outside. Deep in the stove, the coils of the water-back gurgled like a stomach.

"Mom, Irv thinks maybe he isn't qualified to be a fruit tramp at the Oaks. What do you think?"

"Don't let him tease you, Irv. They'll jump at the chance to get a hard worker like you." She brought the big granite-iron coffee pot from the stove and filled his cup.

Bill left the table first to go load the truck. "Good chow, Mom," he said. She handed him two bulging lunch bags. Irv finished his coffee standing up, and hugged her on his way out.

The sun had only half cleared Konocti's south shoulder, its rays not yet reaching down to the unstirring orchards and the pale, empty roads. Irv sat with his hands between his knees, leaning forward and staring straight through the windshield.

"What if he asks if I know how to—whatever it is?"

"Just nod. I'll show you."

The truck had no top or doors. Its sides were open to the floorboards of weathered gray, cracked oak, and its flat windshield, split horizontally, was pushed open for speed. The steady downgrade from the Rincon to Big Valley was slight, but enough to make the truck run easy. It bounced along the tops of the washboard corrugations the county roadscraper left in the gravel.

As the light brightened, thin strips of shade from a line of poplars along the fence slid over their two figures faster and faster, till the truck seemed to be leaping from one shadow to the next. They were giddy with noise and speed. Irv held onto the seat with both hands. When Bill had to brake hard to enter the creek, they let themselves pitch forward, faces shining with triumph, as if they were kids. Irv watched tiny fish like bits of shadow darting out of the way in the water that rippled almost level with his shoes.

When they were clear of the town, he put his feet on the dash and leaned his head back to watch the trees and the sky.

"Nice, huh?" Bill said

"Gosh, I'll say—wonderful. Wouldn't it be a kick if I could have my own place near yours someday?"

Bill turned to stare at him, his hazel eyes glinting under his raised brows. "Are you kidding?" He took his foot off the gas abruptly, so the question seemed to hang in the air. "Almost every ranch in the gulch is teetering on the edge of foreclosure. These lean-acre layouts don't support you, you have to support them. This is a great place to be poor, of course, but that's what it amounts to."

"Wow," Irv said. "That sure backfired. I didn't know you hated it like that."

"Trouble is I don't. I like it. I just know better."

"Lake County may not satisfy you, but I don't have your big-shot aspirations."

"I'd better have aspirations. Look, the folks aren't going to be able to make it much longer, you can see that. I'm going to have to help them, and $4 a day wages won't cut it. Almost everybody in the gulch is working two jobs, and praying for good weather." As they got closer to the lake, the huge shadow of Konocti engulfed them, and the breeze was chill. Irv had tensed up again.

"That's it," Bill tilted his head to indicate two big pillars of field stone that marked the sides of a driveway into the orchard of trees, big, for pears, showing fruit much too green for harvesting. A quarter of a mile farther on he turned the truck into a dusty lane and bounced to a stop beside a bunch of ramshackle cars and trucks at the orchard's edge. A few men were unloading stiff tarps, iron gray and stained, to spread under the best trees to protect the windfalls. The super was allotting clippers on a long pole to the gathering crews.

"This isn't the regular job," Bill said. "I've never done it either. They're thinning some of the heaviest loaded trees. Pampering the jumbos, probably for friends, or exhibitions or something."

A flivver jounced into the yard, crowded with faces and bristling with men on the running boards, hanging on wherever they could. It was the daily sport of those who walked to work from camps to ride the last few hundred yards with the swells who arrived by car. They dropped off like singed fleas when the flivver stopped. Those inside unbent and crawled out. As more men gathered they greeted one another, but so briefly it seemed to Irv they were using some code they all knew.

They weren't young men; nobody seemed young as Bill and him. Some wore overalls and blue shirts, some wore thin shiny-bottomed black suit trousers. Their hats were mostly drooping felt with hat bands stained in odd patterns, one in rolling dark waves, one, a shadowy row of Christmas trees, as though each man's sweat had stained his band with his personal emblem. Bill had given Irv his straw hat for the day and went bareheaded, himself. The manager wore a wide brimmed soft Panama.

A cool somnolence hung on in the orchard still partly under the shadow of the mountain. A lark sat on a split wood fence post facing the men and singing grandly. Each group stopped by the foreman briefly before they faded into the orchard shade. He wore jodhpurs, an open white shirt, and leather puttees. Irv wondered sulkily if he expected to run into snakes or what.

"This is Irv, the new man I mentioned," Bill told him.

"Irv," the foreman acknowledged. "Take him with you for the day, will you Bill? See Harry for some tools."

Irv followed Bill to get a set of the implements the others carried. Bill might say all it took to get hired this time of year was to be alive, but still he was so glad to really get a job, he felt like he had springs on his shoes when he walked. Judging from the even, quiet progress into the orchard, the other men were glad to be there too. They looked wiry and hard-bitten, but they were quick to laugh at cues they all knew. Their shirt sleeves mostly were rolled up over muscles that looked like they'd done plenty of work.

Irv had his sleeves let out down to his hands. As he walked he unbuttoned the cuffs and rolled the sleeves up to his own biceps, red and sore looking, but respectably bulging and scrawled with veins. When he lifted the long tree hooks the pull felt good. Maybe thinning pears didn't take brains, but it took some muscle. He had enough, and he intended to keep up with these tough scrawny buzzards if it killed him.

Bill wore old cords and a faded tan shirt. Irv could remember those cords clear back to high school, the purple stain on the knee was from Chemistry class, and Bill wore them as though they were a badge of office. Still, it was easy to imagine Bill in the jodhpurs and Panama.

Bill enjoyed the quiet deployment into the trees, purposeful as a good machine. Every piece of real machinery on the place ran like that too, nothing makeshift. I've had enough makeshift to last me a lifetime already, he thought. Winton's were artists at it. The Oaks was run like a big outfit, and it made money, but it was unique, a rich man's toy. It was the big spreads in the San Joaquin and Imperial Valley that really turned out the goods, with giant machinery and plenty of Mexicans anxious to come in over the border when their labor was needed. The farmers-by-accident who ended up in Lake County weren't cut out for the work at all, or for any other, for that matter.

Every few rows of trees, a five gallon water bucket stood on a box in the shade. Bill noticed that at one of the buckets, six men were standing, all listening to a big red haired man with a mustache. No one he recognized. He didn't look like one of the workers, somehow, though he was wearing jeans and a work shirt. If he wasn't working for the Oaks, be didn't belong in the orchard. There was no excuse for that many men to be standing around one pail, not even drinking, for listening. The men liked to stall all they could when they went for water, which was O.K. if they didn't overdo it; that was their privilege. He'd give them another minute or so, but if the guy was pedaling some old IWW stuff, he'd see that he moved on.

Bill walked toward the group with the deliberate gait be had. Some of the men moseyed off to their rows again.

"Can I do something for you?" he asked the intruder briskly.

"I just needed to have a word with someone I heard was working here, name of Roy Deines."

Bill scanned the crew quickly. "Roy should be here. Do you want me to tell him who's looking for him when he shows up?"

"No, thanks." The man's voice was unhurried. He stopped to watch while the driver of the water wagon picked up the empty buckets from the rows the crew had worked, and hosed fresh water into one of the buckets ahead of them. "That's a good water arrangement you have," he added, starting to move off again.

"Works out very well," Bill said crisply. Over a dipperful of water, he watched the stranger walk off down the row, stopping for a moment to say something to one of the men .

"I couldn't tell which one he was talking to, could you?" he asked Irv.

"Good Lord, does it matter?"

"Not particularly, but sure, everything matters," Bill said.

Irv regarded Bill for a long moment with a look of puzzlement. "What did he want?" he asked. "My job?"

Bill laughed at him. "No, you're safe. He wouldn't say what he wanted, except to see Roy Deines."

"Who's he?" Irv asked.

Just one of the men with a little more brains than the others."

By afternoon, Irv was so tired he felt as if his gravity had doubled and the whole earth was a sweet invitation to lie down. His shirt clung to his back and shoulders, founding dark blue islands where it was wet with sweat. He had unrolled his sleeves so that the cuffs hung over his hands to save him from more sunburn, and had pulled Bill's hat so far down on his head that its straw peak was almost flattened. In its shadow his face looked thin and strained.

49

Sweat dropped from the end of his nose. The sun radiated from a sky bare of the least wisp of cloud. The men steadily circled the trees, setting up flurries in the leaves as they culled the small or imperfect fruit, and the crews spiraling movement down the long rows was stately as an ocean whirlpool's. Irv worked stolidly, covering the constant battle he had to control the unwieldy tool. While he was maneuvering to clip away a cluster of numerous small fruit half obscured by the thick scratchy leaves and twigs that grasped at his arms and brushed his face, his grip slipped. A clump of pears, some of the biggest on the tree, already showing a touch of dark red on their cheeks, battered down on his head and shoulders. As he ducked to protect his head with his arms, the flopping tool knocked down another heavy shower. They should pay me to rest, he thought, but he kept on angling for the elusive misshapen runts still safe in the high branches, hoping he'd be judged for the bustle he was making, instead of his results. He was dog tired, and had a chain of sore spots at his waist where he had propped the tool to ease his arms. His skin was nettled with a thousand small scratches.

By the end of the day he was stunned with work. When he heard the quitting whistle, he sat down on the clods where he was, and watched the others curiously as they drained down the row toward the tall oaks at the orchard's edge. They looked hot, but not as if they were hurting. Some of the men nodded or looked friendly as they passed. "First day's a bitch, ain't it," one said. When Bill came, Irv joined the trek to the trees.

They headed west when they got out to the road, but where the orchard ended, Bill turned abruptly into a dirt lane that threaded through the tall trees and undergrowth along the creek where a scattering of ragged and stained canvas tents sheltered.

"I have to check on Roy," Bill said. "He didn't show up for work, and I need him tomorrow. I won't be a minute." Irv saw him stop by a boy chopping kindling outside one of the tents, who got to his feet to direct him, pointing deeper into the trees, and gesturing a sharp turn to the right. Bill disappeared in the trees.

Straight ahead from the truck, Irv watched a solidly built woman with a friz of gray hair washing herself at a white enameled basin on an upended pear lug. After a glance at Irv, she ignored him as completely as if he were one of the buckeye bushes, lathering a wash rag and methodically scrubbing her round red face, her ears, her neck and down the unbuttoned front of her dark calico dress into the sunburned cleft between her heavy breasts, rinsing the rag and repeating the process thoroughly again.

A tiny girl came skipping through the stony camp dust in a white cambric shirtwaist and panties. She backed up to the woman confidently to have her backdrop unbuttoned, and skipped off again without a word. "Don't you peepee near the creek," the woman called after her. She slung the wash water alongside the tent in a high glittering arch. The earth where it fell already had a pearly build-up on it.

A couple of men were building a shed with scrap lumber. Irv deduced it was to be a two-holer. Tents, some of them sizable army tents, were strung out between the road and the creek. At one place near the creek he could see old canvas tacked up from tree to tree and rigged with a square five gallon kerosene can for a shower. Smoke was beginning to rise from a few stove pipes angling up from tent sides, and at one battered iron range set up outside on the pebbles, an old woman was turning sizzling sausages that filled the leafy shade with a tantalizing smell.

Bill came back and jumped into his seat, and took off. "Cleared out. You can't depend on even a good fruit tramp," he said.

"You mean he left these swell accommodations? They put up their mules better on this place. Maybe they let him into the barn."

Bill laughed. "One day's work, and you're a Wobbly? Come on, Irv. Free water and free camp sites, what do you want for a nickel.

They live the way they want, and think they're beating the system when they get their kids in school a few weeks without paying taxes anywhere.

They jounced down the lane and toward town in silence. Bill was wondering who he would draft to fill Roy's place. He glanced over at Irv, curiously. "You O.K.?" he asked. "The worst is probably over, though your muscles may be sore for a day or so."

"I'm fine," Irv said. Bill wondered if Irv sounded curt because be was bushed, or if be was still nursing his new IWW sympathies. He'd get the picture when he had a little more experience, Bill concluded.

Chapter 7

Saturday Irv came for Beth in the Wintons' car, dressed in ice cream flannels, with a navy blue blazer. His hair, yellow silk, combed straight back, shone with pomade. He knocked, and heard Beth call out, "Get it for me, will you, Ma?"

Instead of Mrs. Hafner, a stocky man in iron gray work clothes and broad brownish suspenders loomed inside the screen door. He had handsome features, clipped gray hair, and a thick neck with a heavy-skinned vein pulsing regularly into sight. The deep smile lines in his face lay unactivated.

"Huh," he said when he saw Irv. "What's happened to Bill now?"

"He had to go into Calistoga." Irv's voice sounded despicably weak to his own ears. "We thought Beth could go to the dance with me instead."

Frank Hafner's expression made it clear he had given up expecting anything good of Beth's admirers. He turned his head aside and hollered "Babe!" with a threatening rise at the end. He did not unhook the screen.

Irv stood waiting. This man didn't look like the Frank the Wintons had talked about, who sang Italian opera at parties and danced alone with his arms raised, like a Greek, and played elaborate practical jokes. This man was no joker, he was a prick. Beth edged into the doorway beside him, flipped up the hook, and pushed the screen open.

"This is Irv, Pa." Her tone was placating. Irv held out his hand politely. Perfect little gentleman, Hafner thought.

He said nothing. Beth eased through the door to join Irv. "He gets like that, sometimes," she said lamely, as Irv took her elbow and helped her into the Nash.

"I didn't see how he could get that sore at me already."

"You don't know Pa." She answered lightly, but he heard a scared shake in her voice. They drove through the valley in the soft dark. Beth rode looking straight out the windshield, though there were no other cars, and nothing to see. Finally, she let out a giggle and relaxed all at once. She hooked her arm through Irv's.

"Hey, he really scares you, doesn't he," Irv said.

"When he loses his temper, sure. Not now."

Irv slowed down as they got close to one of the red lights, seemingly in the middle of the road, that marked the right angle turns on the way to Lakeport, and Beth told him a town joke, about the outsider that had speeded up there saying, "Watch me pass him," and sailed into the orchard a few feet below.

Irv looked down at her and smiled, thinking how pretty she was, how natural—the way her waist caved in when she laughed, she got so carried away—the way she lifted her face like an offering. He wished he was a foot taller and that he could talk better, like Bill.

The evening air softened with the scent of water as they began to skirt the unseen lake. "What's that smell?" he asked.

"It's a froggy smell," Beth said firmly, not knowing either.

"Do frogs smell? You wouldn't think they would with all that swimming."

"I don't know. It just seems places you hear frogs smell like that. There's lots of tules at this end of the lake, maybe that's it.

"I haven't anything against frogs. It's a kind of fresh smell, only it goes to the bottom of your lungs." He drew in a deep breath, testing.

The nonsense made Beth feel reckless and safe at the same time. She didn't have to be careful what she said to Irv, the way she did with Bill. She guessed that was the way it was when you got all wrapped up in somebody like she was in Bill.

She teased Irv. "When you said you worked nights and Sundays at the country club, I thought you would know all about the country."

"Not this kind of country." Irv laughed and shook his head.

"Is the club nice?" Beth asked.

"Oh, I guess so. It's pretty fancy." He told her about dances at the country club, with potted palms screening little tables with flowers and shaded candles on them, and waiters gliding around, and the women's beaded dresses glittering even when the lights were dim. It surprised him how much he remembered once he started telling Beth.

"It sounds beautiful."

"I suppose it is," Irv said, "or would be if the people there weren't such jerks."

"What's wrong with them?"

With Beth beside him everything about the club seemed rottener than ever. "I'm not sure you want to hear about the people at the country club," he said primly.

For some reason, she felt a wave of gratitude. She laughed and leaned her head against his shoulder. Irv bent his head down to touch the top of hers, but kept his eyes on the road. His shadowy profile looked very serious.

At the dance hall door he paid for a blurry purple stamp mark on his wrist, and he and Beth entered the duskiness of the old Town Hall now used for the dances. It was lit by bulbs hung from the rafters, some bare, some glowing dimly inside paper lanterns. Spindly twists of crepe paper sagged between them. The band was tuning up in a tangle of sounded "A's" and arpeggios, with a few spurts of music rising here and there then sinking back into busy noise.

Beth scanned the hall quickly, looking for someone she hoped she wouldn't find. No Earl, she decided with relief. It would be just like him to show up later, though, and act as if she belonged to him, but Irv probably wouldn't notice. She, herself, could tell just by the way people would get into a car together whether they had also gotten into bed, but she thought maybe that was just the way her mind worked.

A few groups were scattered around the edge of the dance floor. Irv hesitated and asked Beth, "Where do we go?"

"It's just like the geography." She waved toward the north end of the hall. "Upper Lake people stay up there, Lower Lake's at the other end, Lakeport's by the entrance, and Kelseyville's in the middle. Now you know all. Wait a second, while I put my jacket down." She put her things on a chair in Kelseyville territory. The girls there gathered around her saying her maroon accordion-pleated skirt was darling, and asking who the new man was and where was Bill?

An intent silence focused on her answer. Nobody was indifferent to Bill; even the ones who said he was a snob envied her Bill's attention.

"Oh, Irv is an old friend of Bill's up here for a visit. Bill had to go to Calistoga," Beth told them gracefully, as if it were all simple. She complimented one of the girls on her new hairdo, and the subject of Bill was closed, at least while she was there.

The band had begun to play, haphazardly, as though it hadn't decided how it wanted to sound, yet. People seemed to be waiting for something that hadn't happened, except for a few regulars who chatted and did as they pleased, as easy as though they were in their own front yards. Gradually, as more dancers moved on to the floor, the dusky light began to seem warm and secret, and the music's beat took control. Men crossing the floor to choose from the clusters of girls moved with more urgent steps. At the breaks, dancers clapped, laughing and insistent, standing where they were on the floor till the music started up again. The side-by-side stroll of the casual dancers meshed with the twirls and swoops of the Lindy Hop a lot of the others were trying to learn as though the whole wheeling movement on the floor was planned. It was turning out to be a good dance,

Beth and Irv let themselves gravitate out to the edge of the maelstrom, where the movement was sluggish and they could talk as they danced, or sometimes, stand almost still, swaying as they talked.

At one corner, Irv felt Beth stiffen. As he turned he saw a gang of men he hadn't noticed before standing together, some taking swigs out of unlabeled bottles, laughing at one man who was telling a story. One of the men, tall, with a bland face and easygoing muscles raised his bottle in a lazy salute to Beth as they passed by. "Hi, Babe," he said in a level, deliberate tone. Irv recognized him, then. It was the guy that drove Beth's old man home the night before. Earl Green, Umps said his name was. Beth didn't answer him or smile, but his tone wasn't one that just meant, "Hi, Babe," in general, he obviously knew her. The band settled down to "Melancholy Baby." Beth and Irv quit talking and looking around, and just danced.

Beth hadn't imagined that he would be such a good dancer because there wasn't anything showy about Irv. He was wonderful to dance with, easy to follow just by the way be moved. It felt like the music was inside of them. She would give her head a little, abstracted shake, as if she couldn't be interrupted in this silent conversation with Irv when other men came to cut in. Finally when she said she had to accept one, Irv turned to the women on the sidelines and offered himself politely to the nearest.

He noticed Earl cut in on Beth imperiously after she had taken only a few steps with the other partner, and saw Beth turn her face sharply away from his. She danced with a fixed and guarded look on her face.

When the music dictated it, Beth switched out away from Earl expertly. Her dark red accordion pleats flashed and swirled. When they closed, she hissed in his ear, "I told you to stay away from me, and I mean for good. Don't act as though you owned me, either, or I'll walk off the floor right now."

"Afraid your new boyfriend will get a bad impression?" He twirled her around elaborately, looking down, with lazy amusement. "This little stooge isn't even the boyfriend, is he."

"He's no stooge, he's a friend." Her face felt stony. She couldn't have gotten a smile on it if she had to. Anybody she knew would notice she looked queer. She thanked God Bill wasn't even in the county, he was so quick to pick up on things. "Just stay away from Irv, too." She didn't want Irv to drop some remark to Bill about Earl and her that Bill could work on.

In response, Earl laughed and lowered his hands to cup her buttocks and scoop her body against his. On the next twirl away, she jerked her hand free and quickly headed off toward the ladies' room, smiling apology as she wound through dancers, hoping Irv hadn't seen the fight, and wondering what in God's name she could tell him that he would believe if he had. Irv caught a glimpse of her from a distance. He moved to go to her, but stopped because he had a feeling she wouldn't want him to. Whatever the fuss with Earl was about, he could see she didn't want it to show.

Beth ran the last few steps to the ladies, locked the door of a booth, and sank on the closed toilet seat as though she had reached sanctuary. She rested her face in her hands, trying to get calmed down, and wondering how she had ever gotten mixed up with a crum like Earl.

It was as much Pa's fault as anything. He brought Earl home with him from a construction job at one of the resorts when she was still in high school. The way they talked and laughed, she could see they were cronies, in spite of the age difference, and instead of being mean, the way he was with the other boys who came to the house, Pa practically rolled out the red carpet when Earl came to take her to the movies. He had dinner at the house a lot, and had drunk a lot of beer with Pa by the time he took her to a dance at Lower Lake. That night on the way home, he turned off the road onto a single dirt track and drove quite a ways into the pine woods. She remembered how white and drained the moon looked. It made her feel like they were in a strange forsaken place, a million miles from nowhere. They petted a lot more than she ever had before, but when he started going down her neck and up her skirt and tried to push her down on her back, she had jumped up and said he had to take her right home. He had sat looking stubborn, straight ahead, and then laughed as though he was disgusted but he had driven her home like she told him to.

It was a way over a month before he showed up again, and then it was for dinner with the family, like at first. When finally they did go to a dance in town, Earl had gotten so drunk she had to drive home. He'd fallen asleep in the truck so she covered him up and left him in it. He was softly snoring.

The next time. they went out and were necking, Earl got a comforter out of the back of the truck and slammed the tail gate hard and spread the quilt on the pine needles and pulled her out to it. He was laughing at her for being a virgin, teasing her and coaxing her, sort of, but the way he pinned her down when she pretended to try to get away wasn't kidding.

At school after that, when some girl in the dressing room would be giggling and worrying whether a monkey bite on her neck would show when they put on gym suits, she would be wondering where she and Earl would make love this time when he picked her up after school. It was all she could think about, the way they would do it next. At school dances when a younger kid would cut in on her and would blush when he got excited and dance wide apart from her so she wouldn't notice she had almost laughed. They seemed like babies.

She could hardly wait from day to day to see Earl. Then his work got scarce and he started to hang around with a bunch of other loafers at the pool hall, and didn't hardly have money enough to buy gas. He got so he would come to the house, way late at night, and tap at her window and she would let him in through it. She was always scared what Pa might do if he ever discovered them.

She would rather use any other place, even the deserted shed out in the brush where they went a lot, but somehow she always ended up doing just as Earl wanted, though she was so scared she didn't even enjoy it any more, it went on like that, and when she heard Earl had taken some Lower Lake girl home from a dance he hadn't asked her to, she blew up and told him she didn't want to go with him any more.

The smell of the toilets seemed to get strong suddenly, and she felt sick at herself, huddling in there. She combed her hair quickly, and fled the place to find Irv again.

It was so easy with Irv. She just said she wanted to go outside for a minute, and they did. She couldn't have passed that long an absence off like that if it had been Bill. She almost laughed with relief as she took Irv's arm to steady herself in her high heels when they went out on the stepping stones to a big rock in the water. Frogs sawed away loud as an orchestra. The sky looked misty, there were so many stars, but you could see farther and farther into them the longer you looked. Irv said he'd never seen so many.

He didn't say anything about the dance, or about her, so Beth knew he had seen her getting away from Earl, and how she felt, and that he wouldn't ask about it. Or talk about it either. What she'd been afraid of was that somebody would tell Bill. She knew now it wouldn't be Irv. On the way back to the dance floor, she could feel his heart pounding just holding his arm, and she thought she knew the exact minute he would have kissed her if she hadn't been Bill's girl. For a little while, she forgot that the mess with Earl ever happened.

They strolled over for a drink at the long table where punch and pop were sold with their little fingers linked. Earl was nowhere in sight. Beth made her skirt ripple as she turned to take the drink Irv offered her. Irv watched her over the tepid punch in his glass. He noticed the dazzled brightness of her eyes and thought it was almost like the way the women at the club, the younger ones, would look when they were getting tight, a kind of bewildered radiance. But there sure wasn't anything in that punch to make anyone radiant.

With Beth it was just natural. He danced with his cheek against her dark hair. It smelled like the dewy grass that had brushed his ankles when they walked down to the lake. Later, as some of the older ones left for bed, high school kids would jump up and yank at the faded crepe paper streamers. Irv and Beth waltzed past the open windows, the breeze soothed his burning face the way Beth's cool fingers had when she put salve on his sunburn.

At two o'clock, when the band launched into "Let Me Call You Sweetheart," for the last set, Earl pushed his way through to them on the dance floor. "How about me having the last dance, Babe," he said. His voice was rough; he was standing close to Beth, looking down at her. He ousted Irv with his shoulder, and grabbed Beth's hand to pull her to him. "Don't worry, kid, I'll bring her back," he said over his shoulder to Irv as he swung away with Beth. Irv stumbled backward against a chair, and then launched himself.

"Leave her alone," he yelled, banging Earl's shoulder to break him away from Beth. Earl held her tighter and swung her around so she was between Irv and him. She twisted clear of Earl then, and Irv lowered his head and pounded into Earl's belly with fast, close punches like he was working out on a dummy. Earl bent forward with his air knocked out of him, and Irv landed a smack on his chin. Earl's face registered that he didn't believe what was happening to him, but that he would soon fix it. He straightened and drew back his arm with intent to kill, but his elbows were caught in a grip solid as cement. Outraged, he twisted his neck around to see a big red-haired man grinning as he held him frozen. A couple of men grabbed Irv, and others came to take over Earl. It was dance etiquette for other men to break up scuffles on the floor so the whole dance wouldn't bust up. Both the fighters were still struggling furiously to get back to the battle. Some men from the crowd were hurrying to get into the scene. One, dark and aquiline, jerked his face away from the light as soon as he recognized Scott, faded back into the crowd out of sight. The others hesitated.

Scott moved in beside Irv. "Why don't you take Beth home now, Irv," he said evenly.

Irv remembered seeing him at the swimming hole, remembered the scar on his back. Beth said, "Please, Irv." Irv, glassy-eyed, still struggling, stopped and nodded solemnly, and they left slowly along the edge of the floor, while the orchestra took a winding modulation down for the last chorus, with the lights dimmed to just two big spots wandering bumpily over the quiet heads of the crowd.

Chapter 8

First she'd get the wash done and hung out, Viv told Stevie who was loading empty soap cartons into his wagon. She'd make Izzy's cake later, after lunch, Devil's Food with walnut fudge frosting. Her sixteenth birthday would be more grown-up, maybe, but it wouldn't change Izzy's preference for double chocolate. She was still the same child.

She had the first load of wash going already. The washing machine stood on the screened porch on bandy legs beside the cement stationary tubs, sunbursts of morning light glancing from its varnished copper sides. The clothes were tugged harshly back and forth by the new "whale tail agitator," as the Sear's Roebuck catalog called it. She dipped into the tub to pull a heavy towel up to the wringer. To get the sopping wad through it, she leaned so heavily on the crank that a fringe of her loosened hair came close to tangling in the rubber rollers. She lifted her arm to brush the hair away from her face with the crook of her elbow. Stevie, loading empty soap cartons into his wagon, watched, his gray-blue gaze steady. For a long moment the elbow hid her face in a classic posture of grief. Stevie stopped loading. She straightened and slowly swept her arm upward, revealing a dazzling smile, and eyes sparkling at the joke. Stevie chuckled, and got busy with his boxes again.

Viv picked up the basket heaped with wrung-out wash and shoved the screen door open with a hip. "Bring the clothespins, will you, Honey?"

He dumped out the cartons and reloaded the wagon with the lumpy green gingham clothespin sack to follow her out to the back shed where the lines were strung on rickety poles planted in hard-packed earth. When she got an ear of a pillowcase or a shirt tail raised to the line, Stevie reached her the pins to fasten it. Their pace picked up when they came to a nest of socks in the basket, and slowed to normal for a batch of dish towels. A heavy bath towel pulled away from her fingers while she was hoisting it up, but Stevie clutched it to his sturdy little body with both arms as it slid past him, rescuing all but a tag end from the dirt.

"You sure are my right hand man, Stevie," Vivian said, kneeling to take it from him and to rub her cheek against his. "Look," she pointed to the steam rising from the line, "we got those clothes hung up so quick they're smoking."

"Yeah," Steve said with satisfaction.

"Rabbits, next, then I've got to get Izzy's birthday cake going. O.K.?"

"O.K." he said.

Steve strode among the hutches in the barn on his sturdy child's legs like an overseer. Helping with the rabbits was his favorite chore. He liked lifting the animals by their stiff velvet ears, but he also noticed what they liked and what they didn't, and what ways worked best with them. Viv often told him the rabbits rambunctious success was more his doing than hers. She had mixed feelings about the rabbits.

Steve was hardly more than a baby when he first saw an ancestor of the present rabbit in a wire crate on the barn floor. He had toddled around the big white bunny, and watched it, twinkling and nibbling in the cage, with dazed admiration. When he poked his finger through the wire top to touch its soft white coat, the red-eyed buck stood up on its back legs to sniff it, and then bit it, hard. Vivian still winced, remembering the shock and pain on Steve's face, and his blood dripping into the hay. She had rocked him to her, assuring him that the rabbit thought his finger was a carrot, and though Stevie had believed and forgiven, she never quite forgave rabbits. It made it easier on her when she had to send them to market.

Steve climbed up on a high stool at the wooden kitchen table to crack the walnuts for her while she sifted flour and beat eggs for Isobel's birthday cake. With both hands on the nut cracker he still couldn't faze them, and when he banged them with a hammer they shot out from under his blows and skidded into the corners. Patiently he captured a nut between the cracker's jaws, then holding it down like quarry, hammered it open. He raised his head to look up at Viv. She nodded to show she admired his solution.

She stirred the batter in the brown-striped yellow ware bowl, and poured it into the pans. "There's a little extra," she said, "Do you want to lick it or shall I make a man?"

"Make a man," Steve said.

She scraped the last of the batter into a gingerbread form. Stevie watched the fellow lying on the table in the small bright coffin while Vivian gave him black currant eyes and a surprised round currant mouth.

"Put a dinky on him," he said.

"Batter isn't like pie dough, Stevie, it won't stay put. Let's see, though—" she stirred the pile of broken shells with her forefinger till she found bits of walnut meat with the right convolutions, and put them in place. Steve smiled, satisfied.

Isobel had done the breakfast dishes and fed and watered the chickens on her way to the Wilkes place early enough that she could feel the sun hot on one ear while the other was still cool. She especially felt like swimming, and hoped she and Jeanne could have the Wilkes pond to themselves a while. Pear season was almost here, and once that started everything else took second place. In fruit season you had to work when the fruit was ready; what you wanted to do didn't matter. She wanted to swim and play till she was tired of it, while she could. At the bottom of the Wilkes land, the creek spread in the sun to a broad shallow pool altogether different from the swimming holes higher up. Here no trees hung over the water to shade it. It got warm earlier, and the sandy bottom had some big stones and that made good hiding places for their game. It was a place even the small children could swim safely without grown ups around. All the kids gathered there for early swims whenever they could. She didn't feel like playing the hide-the-golfball game, though. The last time she did that, she'd put all the balls she found into one of the little kids' hidden pile. She didn't want to be the winner, she was too big. It wouldn't be right.

Jeanne Winton and some small boys from ranches upstream were there already, as well as three of the Wilkes children who were still young enough to be free on a summer day. They hadn't gone down to the creek yet when Izzy arrived, but were playing Run Sheep Run, tearing around the yard in front of the barn, and in the corn field below a bank, where they carefully skirted Mr. Wilkes truck garden laid out in plots and marked with string tied with strips of white cloth issuing a blanket "Keep Off" warning to all species. It worked. Nobody doubted Mr. Wilkes was serious when he said something, which was seldom. The garden was the best in the gulch. It made money. The children never stole so much as a green pea.

Kate Wilkes was ironing on her screen porch at the back of the house, her lanky figure straightening often so she could watch the children play. A pale, plain woman, with mole-brown hair in flat loops beside her face and done up in a small knot at her neck, she was whimsical about her looks and her lot in life, and patient and good-natured with the neighborhood children, as well as her own. She wanted to get her ironing done before the heat took hold. She could tell already that the day was going to be a scorcher. The sky had that

high endless blue look, and she could feel beads of sweat at her hair-
line already.

She called Isobel over to her and asked her to be sure to stop in
before she went home. She had a little packet she wanted her to take
to her mother. Izzy said she would, and went back to the game, or at
least she went to join Jeanne where she was hiding in the lilacs by the
porch steps.

Chapter 9

Last of the supper dishes, Viv washed up the cake pans, wiping them with a little oil, so they wouldn't rust. There, Izzy's birthday. When it came and went, you knew where you were in the year—right at the peak, in full blown summer. There would be no more throwback times, like in the spring, when the weather would renege on its promises and turn dark and cold. From now on, summer weather, days, so long it seemed like time got lazy, overblown. There was time to burn, plenty of everything, especially time, just dip into the big bowl. That was what summer still said, even though every summer it seemed like they had to work harder and faster and longer. There was a hitch somewhere.

Not everybody felt the way she did about summer, she finally realized. So, rather than be unsociable she laughed and agreed the heat was awful when people complained about it, but even when her face felt like it would burst and her eyes got that funny desperate look from the heat, never mind what she might look like, she felt supple and easy in her body, and she could do twice as much work. Summer days started off full swing, instead of everybody huddling and stalling half the morning till they got warmed up. She loved summer as much as the kids did. They got brown and healthy, and she didn't have to worry about them.

She hung up the dishpan. No sound of Stevie. She pushed open his door and saw him face down in his crib, with the sides up. Probably he'd put them up himself and climbed in over the end.

In the kitchen she put her palm to the side of the galvanized water heater to see how much hot was left for her bath. She started the water running in the tub, brushed her teeth, cleaned the basin. The bath water was still shallow, but the placid sound of it was soothing. She wasn't in a hurry, she had done all she could for the day.

Tomorrow, she supposed she'd better start Izzy's new dress if she expected to get it done before the pears came in. She pulled out her tortoise shell pins and let her hair tumble shining to her waist. It was silky in her hands as she wound it on top of her head for the bath. Just that little bit of vinegar in the rinse did that. In the mirror above the basin she glimpsed the admiration in her own eyes, and smiled back acknowledgment of the compliment as she'd learned to do when she was young and everybody told her how pretty she was. She sure didn't get much practice doing that lately.

The water pipe croaked as she nipped off the water, starting to run cool though there was only a few miserable inches in the long tub. The tub, standing on legs too short for its length, seemed to sag in the middle like a dachshund. Viv always felt it should have a more substantial underpinning, like a hippopotamus. When they first moved in, Charlie offered to put boots on its legs if it bothered her too much.

She had to slide down flat on her back with her neck bent almost at right angles against the tub to get much of her under the lapping water. She surveyed the length of her body wavering white under the ripples, breasts and knees rising from the water like islands, circled by island waves. She watched the hair of her bush lift and sway like seaweed as a wave reached it. She brushed both stranded nipple peaks. Poor neglected beauties, so used to attention when Charlie, and then the babies thought you were the wonders of the earth, and couldn't get enough of you. No more. Charlie was always in a hurry now, as though he was behind schedule even in bed. Touchy. If I dare draw his hand to favor them, he acts insulted. Thanks me not to interfere.

The towel waiting on the chair looked dingy and limp. She took it in both hands and dipped her head to sniff it: sweet as sun and wind, just gray from too many water-stingy washes. She wished once she could get out of the tub and wrap herself in a big showy white towel, like the ones that hung on the rods in the Borg's bathroom, beside their pure white unstained, unringed wash basin. She couldn't keep her own tub and basin that clean if she died trying. They didn't have it in them any more.

Her cotton flannel bathrobe, washed soft and faded so that the pattern of lavender, peach and tan looked blurred and pretty, felt comfortable as she pulled it on. Then she remembered the parcel Izzy had brought her from Kate Wilkes. She'd been too busy cooking then, and had put it on a kitchen shelf. She went out barefoot to retrieve it, and opened it expecting it to be some produce or herbs Kate wanted her to try. There was white tissue paper inside the brown wrapping, and inside that her fingers hit velvet. White velvet, padded, quilted embroidered slippers, made just her size with fine embroidery on the toes, of pink rabbit eyes, and white whiskers, and long velvet ears lined with pink silk and tied together into a bow. She wiggled her feet into their soft padding, and patted each foot up and down to make the ears flop. Then she walked around the bathroom watching them. The were perfectly made, with tiny even stitches. She could see the hours Kate had put into them. They were works of art, so luxurious she bet some old finery from Kate's family in the East had gone into them. She flapped the ears again. She liked having something comical on her feet.

From the damp, the hair around her face had taken on a darker shade, and clustered into curls. She tipped her head and combed it through, gently, then, in the mirror watched her fingers scampering down her chest on each side from ear to waist braiding it. They knew how to braid perfectly, though she couldn't have described what they did for the life of her. It was a good thing she hadn't let on to Isobel what she thought of it.

She could hear Steve's peaceful breathing as she passed his door on the way to bed. A streak of moonlight was shining clear into the hall from her and Charlie's room, and she could see their window curtains quivering a little in it. Charlie was sound asleep on his side, his head and shoulders hunched over so all that showed was the curly hair on the back of his head, but she could tell his legs were open in a full stride across the foot of the bed. Under the blankets his body looked more like he was pushing into a strong wind than like he was resting. She eased under the bed clothes carefully, so she wouldn't wake him. He wasn't getting the sleep he needed, with his strained back. She felt sorry about his back. It was just one more thing for him to be touchy about. When she ran out to help him carry a sack of feed into the barn, he'd acted as if she'd insulted him. There wasn't anything she could say about it, either.

She could see why he would mind that. He used to be her knight. From the very first, back on the school bus, when any of the kids teased her or jostled her, he would protect her. The time old Mr. Snook drove the bus over the edge of the canyon while he was watching the rear view mirror, Charlie had been in front of her, so it was him that had the scar from breaking glass. Charlie took charge that day just naturally, without thinking about it, telling them all to quit yelling and not move a particle, but stay just where they were. "You too, Snooks," he said to Mr. Snook who did as he was told. They stayed still as stone while he crawled out the window and up the bank and went for a tow truck. When they pulled her up with the ropes, Charlie put his arms around her and held her tight for a minute.

Because of Charlie, the ride on the bus was the best part of going to school She didn't even remember anything abut the two years he was away with his father in Chicago. It was on the bus they first saw each other again. He got in all bent over because he's gotten so tall, but he forgot when he saw her, and raised up and hit his head on the bus roof.

71

"When did you get so pretty!" he said, drawing it out like a whistle and rubbing the spot he'd bumped. She laughed at the memory, and turned on her side to curl her body around his. Wherever he was going with that long stride, she wanted to go too, but the way his leg was stretched back clear across the bed, there was no way she could do it.

In his sleep, Charlie gave an impatient jerk away, then curled up still tighter, drawing his striding legs together and pulling his knees up. Viv lay still as though she was listening for a distant call, then as she drowsed off, curved herself to his back.

A car went by on the road, making a steady low-pitched buzz that faded and was finally cut off by the hill at the Meyer place. A weak wind twisted the leaves on the cottonwood beside the house, and brought a scent of skunk, dilute with distance, but enough to set off a couple of slow, deep barks fetched from old Heide in the barn across the road. Then a long quiet spell till the wind strengthened enough to bang the barn loft door at long, uneven intervals. Thump, thumpthump, silence. Thump, thumpthump.

Charlie lay still with his hands between his knees trying to identify the unease that persisted in his mind, palpable as a sour stomach. He was sore about something. For one thing, he was sore at the way Gloria had acted at the pear shed, watching from her roadster, calm and cool, while he made a pitiful fool of himself unloading the truck. Sat there, smoking idly, like she was watching a race she hadn't any money on.

Last night in town, though, she barged right over to Wint's car the minute she spotted him sitting in it, sure of herself as a cheeky kid. She hadn't minded showing what she thought of him either. A simple smile started on his face, and was scowled off. He certainly didn't intend to let her have the upper hand, here. He would let her know that, politely of course.

He didn't tell Viv that Gloria had been in town. She'd want to know how Gloria looked, and he didn't have the heart to tell her, better than ever. Naturally, he had to admit, it wasn't entirely to save Viv's feelings. He wasn't sure of her reaction, and the last thing in the word he wanted was any more trouble. Of any kind. It had always been all the trouble he could handle just to keep something from Viv, she picked up on things so quick.

He flopped over on his back. That time he had clap, still just a dumb kid. Deserved what we got—how many, seven, eight, maybe, lined up by the shed back of the dance hall, and that poor funny-looking Lower Lake girl, one after another. Made him sick to think of it. What if he and Viv had been sleeping together then. He was scared the story would get around, but it never had. Hard faking, though, feeling and looking like he did. Viv probably never even heard of clap.

He hadn't even said Hello, how are you, when he saw the girl, after. Did they all walk right by her, like him? Shit heels. Might not even have been her had the clap in the first place.

He clasped his hands back of his neck. Gloria acted as though they would take up exactly where they left off all those years ago—still buddies. But Gloria didn't look like anybody's buddy, anymore. More like a flapper in a magazine. Funny, she turned out like that, with that super-efficient fruit-tramp husband she had. She still acted a lot like she used to, but not really. It used to be him that set up their gags in school, but now she was calling the plays, sort of. He could assure her that the last thing on earth he was interested in was any more bosses. He had bosses to burn.

That was another thing he'd kept quiet about to Viv. He hadn't told her about the little talk old Hinkley said they needed to have. Poured him a cup of the awful coffee he kept in his office, and started real fatherly: realized Charlie had difficulties with his back, but people were complaining that they couldn't count on him to be on time, and they had to use their own workers to load and unload. Would Charlie like a hired helper, somebody to ride along with him and do most of the loading? They'd have to work out something in the pay, naturally. It was all he could do to sit there and take it. Frankly, he felt about ready to tell Hinkley to go screw himself.

To top it off, Hinkley complained the ranch was running down under Charlie's care and management. Even if he took the whole prune crop, he said, it wouldn't pay a decent rent on the place. He even hinted that he should get a cut of Viv's profits on the rabbits. Charlie hunched up even tighter and lay still for a long time, his eyes still wide open in the dark.

Chapter 10

Liz moved about the stove, deft and stately in her domain. The water for the pasta had been boiling so long a gleaming skim of mineral had formed on it. Liz glanced at it, a shadow of distaste passed across big clear features, and she put on a fresh kettle-full. When she bent from the waist to poke small splits of wood into the fire box, her broad bottom in her coral and blue print dress bloomed in the kitchen like a big bouquet. Frank was later than usual; he'd want his dinner when he got in from the Springs, it was a long ride. Snaps from the new wood catching fire settled to an ardent purr. She gave the sauce a stir, and relocated it farther off the heat.

From two tall windows at one end of the room, dim evening light still showed, and a white porcelain shade focused a bright cone over the big black kitchen range and made its pierced nickel trim gleam. Against the wall at the opposite end of the room stood the couch where Frank liked to lie listening to the Philco while he waited for his meals. The couch cover was of dark rust and green woven stuff with a pattern blurred now with shadow. A red checked cloth spread catty-corner on the table across from the stove, showed triangles of dark varnished oak.

Beth brought her bottle of Cutex to the kitchen table so she could listen to the radio while she did her nails. She switched on the overhead chandelier and let the news rattle on in ominous tones without paying any attention to it. She was basking in the feeling she

75

had got from the way Irv treated her, that she was worth taking care of. This was different from knowing she was pretty and that men liked her. It kept coming back to her at odd times all day, and on the strength of it she had decided she wasn't going to stand for anything she didn't like from Earl or anybody else from now on.

Liz opened the oven and the big bouquet bloomed again as she bent to turn the meat, which sizzled fiercely for a moment, and sent out a rich, pungent smell. It was almost ready to take out. Liz stood by with composure for the last few minutes it needed, the long two pronged fork ready in her hand. She considered Beth's dark head bent over the little nail polish brush, tenderness softening her full-cut lips and dark eyes.

"You never said anything about the dance. How was it."

"Oh, like always," Beth sounded distant and casual. She didn't see any way she could tell Ma how nice Irv was at the dance without telling her how awful Earl had acted. "Irv was nice."

The radio chirped, "When whippoorwills call, and evening is nigh, I hurry to my—blue—heaven." A truck clattered into the driveway back of the house. "There's your father," Liz said.

Beth knew the sound of the truck well enough, but it wasn't Pa's. Liz went to unhook the screen to the back door in time to open it for Frank, who limped in wincing, supported by Earl's arm around his waist.

"Calm down," Frank said, when Liz began to fuss over him. He avoided the chair she tried to get him to sit down in, and stood propped up by his hands on the table. "I just picked up a sprinkle of rock salt in the backside, that's all. That damnfool caretaker out there hasn't got the brains to handle a water pistol, let alone a shotgun." He sniffed in disgust. "Get me a glass of wine, will you Babe."

Earl finished telling the story. Frank was fixing the flat on his truck in the parking lot after work. A cougar had been seen around at night, and Clem, the watchman claimed he had orders to give it a dose of rock salt to persuade it to clear out. He got Frank instead.

With Liz supporting him under one shoulder, Frank hobbled into the bedroom. She got a basin of water and tweezers and alcohol, and while he sprawled face down on the bed cursing with pain, carefully picked out the embedded crystals. Presently she stopped working, staring at the back of Frank's head. "Cougar, my foot," she thought. Her lips curled back as though she tasted gall. Then she bent again to her task. In the kitchen Earl helped himself to a glass of wine, then reached out suddenly to pull Beth onto his lap as she passed the table. She strained away from him, and braced with her back to the stove, stood regarding him. "You're both lying, aren't you. That silly story—there hasn't been a mountain lion in the county for ten years."

"What do you know about it," Earl said. "It's real mountain country out there. Mountain lion country."

Beth slid the spaghetti into the water which had just hit a rolling boil, and went out to the back porch to get the butter and salad from the ice box.

"You staying for dinner?" she asked without expression.

"I'm staying all night. Your father can't drive in his present condition, remember? I drove him home. His Ford is still in the lot at the Springs with a flat tire."

"Did Pa say you could stay?"

"He just about ordered me to."

Liz and Frank came back into the kitchen moving together like partners in a three legged race. "I'll see you later," Earl murmured to Beth, while they were all sitting down to the table. She didn't even dare look up to show him what she thought of him, for fear the folks would catch on to how mad she was at him. When they had their big bust-up in April, she had pretended it was like the other times when Earl had stayed away awhile, and that she had just as soon he stayed away for good this time. Pa said she sounded like she had the makings of an old maid, even though she was a looker, and Ma just shrugged, but Beth knew she didn't think much of Earl either.

After dinner Liz helped Frank get into the side of the bed usually hers, where it was easier to get in and out. He complained that it didn't seem natural, that he wouldn't be able to sleep that way, but was soon snoring into the big pillows. It was a grand bed, her parents' wedding present to them, of rich wood smooth as ivory to touch with a grain like streaming wind clouds beneath the surface. It and the matching bureau and wardrobe took up most of the space in the room, but Liz loved the big pieces and the curtains of heavy green embossed stuff, edged with a braid hung with little red plush balls like cherries. The bed lamp had a pagoda shaped shade of pink silk. It was the way a bedroom should be. When she was a child she had climbed in between her big parents in just such a bed, Sunday mornings in San Francisco, with the fog horns bellowing below them on the bay.

When she got up onto the bed on the unaccustomed side, it sank with her weight. When she and Frank were first married, she had hardly made any dent at all, she had been so slim. She lay staring at the ceiling wondering whose wife Frank was after now out at the Springs. Frank never fooled around with the neighbor women at home, she'd credit him with that. It was when he went on out-of-town stone mason jobs, she always heard somehow about some escapade. She sighed, remembering when they were first married how Frank would come home for lunch every day and eat in a hurry so he could pull her into the bed before he went back to work. It had hurt her then. She had got so she dreaded the sound of the noon whistle, till Frank said that wasn't the way it should be, and had taken her to see a doctor. Why, she hadn't even known what it felt like until after that little operation, then she began to wait for the noon whistle too. She dozed off, her face peaceful.

Beth did the dishes fast and stalked past Earl, who was listening to Amos and Andy, to her room without saying anything. She slipped her rayon nightgown over her head and sat at her ivory painted dressing table to brush out her hair. She could hear Earl out in the yard shifting tools in his truck and banging the tail gate closed for the night. She remembered Irv checking to see the door was closed safe when he put her into the Nash.

Her mouth in the mirror reflected a pang of emotions. She couldn't figure out whether it was pity or sympathy, or what, or even whether it was for Irv or herself, but she liked the way it made her look. Her dark hair clung to the brush as her stroke gentled. She remembered how graceful she had felt at the dance with Irv, and how he had wanted to fight Earl even if he probably would get almost killed. It made her laugh to think how helpless Earl had been in the hands of that lumberjack. Earl thought he was such big stuff.

At first she had felt there was something not quite natural about Irv being so considerate, till she began to fit into it. Now it made her mad just to think how she used to let Earl treat her. She was glaring into the mirror, so taken up with resentment that for a second she didn't register she really was staring straight into Earl's eyes reflected in the glass. He closed the door softly behind him, holding her gaze. She felt like throwing the brush at him. "I told you to stay out of here," she said, trying to keep Pa and Ma from hearing, but so mad she hissed like an alligator. Earl came up behind her and crossed his arms over her shoulders, a hand cupping each breast.

"I swear I'll call Ma." Her jaws were clenched with fury. She could see he was standing with one foot curled behind the other, casual, as if nothing she could do would bother him a bit.

"You wouldn't do that, would you," he said in a teasing voice. Beth turned around to face him, and tried to hit him with the brush, but he snagged her wrist, and twisted it till she had to drop it. She beat him with her fists but it was discouraging to be hurting herself more than him. She was panting with fury and exhaustion, but he looked cool, and kept a smile on his face, as though this was child's play. He got both wrists behind her in one hand and strained her chin up with the other to kiss her. She managed to wrench away from him, but the struggle had changed. The issue had narrowed, somehow to a hushed, ferocious game. He was above her, his knees pinning her flat while he pulled at his clothes. She watched him silently, seizing the least advantage to twist away, then losing, lay inert as dough as he covered her. He reared back on his arms to peer enquiringly down at her, and with a half-amused frown, cupped his hand and smacked her on the side of the head, just enough to jolt her, as he might a radio that wouldn't play, or a clock he had wound up that refused to start.

Chapter 11

Beulah sighed with relief when Brownie took over and she could sit back altogether and watch the buzzard soaring in the brilliant sky. He looked black and graceful way up like that instead of roughed-up gray brown with a scruffy head and hunched shoulders like she knew he really was. There came another one in from the south. It began to trace the same circle, as though they were riding on opposite sides of a slow-turning wheel. She caught the taint of the dead thing that attracted them, and wondered if they could tell what they were going to have for dinner just by the smell, and if they favored some meals over others, like folks did.

She knew the way to town, but sometimes when she got to thinking too hard about something else, she would forget. She got there with Brownie, though, every Thursday to get the groceries and feed for the stock, and bring Pa his books from the library. There weren't any other horses on the road except occasionally a team hauling a spray rig or a cultivator from one orchard to the next. She didn't want to admit it but it made her feel almost dizzy, not to know where she was, like the ground had fallen away under the wagon and she was floating, she didn't know where, like the buzzards.

As her wagon crept up a rise of land crested with low manzanita, Beulah began to feel things gradually getting more recognizable, like when she was little and would lie across the seat of the swing on her stomach watching the ground pouring by like a stream beneath her and congealing slowly as she lost speed, till when she finally stopped, there was the dust and twigs and pebbles clear and plain as ever.

It was like that as she and Brownie topped the hill. There was Breen's vineyard fresh with new leaves, and down a ways, the straggling line of trees where Kelsey Creek ran, and beyond that Konocti and the circle of hills far back holding the valley inside it, as she should have known. She shook her head and laughed. Imagine thinking she could get lost in her own county. It was probably because she had been thinking so hard about the dress she had to buy.

She would stop at the library for Pa's books, as soon as she got in town, and then she would go have her pie and coffee next, to give her time to work up to Robison's in her mind.

Brownie and the wagon had to stop in the street after they left the library because men were loading branches of a tree that was cut down, into a truck. They stopped right in front of Lucy Hendrick's house and sure enough, Eugene was riding his trike in the front yard, as usual.

It was a big square yard without anything growing in it, which made you notice what a lot of cement-work people in town had in their front yards—a big strip of sidewalk next to the street with a narrower walk down the middle to the front door, and two walks down the sides of the lot, and another one across the front of the house. Eugene was pedaling his big tricycle along the walks, as fast as he could go, his knees pumping up and down almost to his ears.

He was a big tall boy, and though his trike was the biggest one she had ever seen, he was twice as big a boy as she had ever seen on a tricycle at all. He was going so fast that when he turned onto the narrow strips he had to lean way over so that one wheel rose up in the air when he made the turn, almost the way Gyp would lift one of his legs. Then the trike would bang down again on all three wheels, or sometimes he didn't make the turn and would go bouncing off over the hard caked earth of the yard. Not often though.

Because in addition to the cement walks there were lots of pathways he had made with the trike, and usually he could stay on one of them till he got back on his main route.

When he missed everything though, his face would go blurry with the jouncing. He had a round vague face, shiny and pale as the moon when it was still up in the sky during the daytime.

Eugene had to stay in his own yard all the time when Lucy was working at the Post Office. She guessed that was why he made so many paths in his yard. It was too bad he didn't have more room than he did, but he certainly made good use of what he had.

An automobile waiting back of the wagon honked so Beulah and Brownie had to move on. They got their favorite parking place when they turned on to Main Street, the only hitching post left in town, in front of the bandstand. It was an iron pole with a horse's head on top. Beulah liked to hitch Brownie there because it was a place intended for him. He could tie up there just as sure of himself as the cars that rolled up to park at the curb.

She went straight into Tallman's for her pie and coffee. Mr. Tallman wrote down her order, though it was the same every week, and Mrs. Tallman cut her pie generously and put a paper doily under it. Beulah always thought the treat at Tallman's ended off the day in town perfectly, but she could see now it was a good way to start it too.

She was stirring the cream and sugar into her coffee when the preacher came through the door. He walked back through the other tables and stopped at hers. Bowing his head politely he said, "Miss Colson, do you mind if I sit down with you a minute?"

Beulah slopped her coffee over the edge of the cup and put her spoon down loudly. She turned her head away a second to get her composure and then told him, "Certainly, Reverend," as though it was an everyday thing for her to be singled out. She couldn't imagine what to say next. Reverend Harper went on.

"I didn't get a chance to speak with you when I visited your father, but I want to be sure you know about the revival meetings we're having Saturday nights. I hope to see you there next Saturday. A lot of folks come in from along Kelsey Creek, so I'm sure some of your neighbors would pick you up and see you home."

"I—" she started, "Pa—."

"If you'd like to come, just tell Mrs. Tallman here. She's one of our regulars, and she could see about getting the ride for you." He walked up to the counter, contemplating the floor boards, and Beulah could see him talking to Mrs. Tallman.

Beulah hardly knew where to look when she could see that he was coming back to her table. He told her Mrs. Tallman was sure she could get a ride for her Saturday, if she would like. Then he said, "She tells me you and Mr. Sooter are planning to be married. I wish to offer the use of our mission for the ceremony." It sounded very fine and important the way he said it, but Beulah couldn't see herself in the picture somehow, or Jess either. "You want a true wedding in God's sight," Harper continued "not some hole-and-corner contract signed by a judge." He sounded stern.

Beulah thought "hole and corner" was a funny thing to say. That wouldn't be any place for a wedding. So far when she thought about it the wedding was just somewhere with her and Jess in the center and pretty light all around them like sun on a day when there's a breeze blowing.

There was something else, but she couldn't quite place it in her mind. It was like trying to remember exactly what something or other smelled like, peaches, or poppies, for instance. She would almost get it, but she couldn't pin it down. The reverend went on talking in a serious voice while she tried to catch whatever it was that kept escaping her.

When she went into Robinson's Dry Goods and Hardware store, Roy was busy at the dry goods counter, selling some elastic. She could see his hand flashing back and forth along the yardstick glued to the counter, measuring one yard after another as quick as you could say Jack Robinson. She stopped for a minute after she thought that, and then she had to laugh at the joke she had made.

Beulah felt a lot more experienced as a shopper because the last time she was in town she had bought a pair of lady's shoes, as Pa had told her to do, at Macomber's shoe store, and they were fine except she felt tippy in them sometimes because the soles were so much narrower than her boots. She was still partial to her boots because you knew where you stood with them. They never went back on you, where the new shoes were unpredictable in a rounded gutter, or where there were pebbles.

She went to the back of the store where bolt upon bolt of dress goods was stacked up on the shelves from waist high to ceiling. She stood looking up at the stacks for a long while, they were so pretty, going from green to blue and little printed designs, then plain colors again.

Somebody else was over back of the clothes racks winding up the Victrola there and playing records.

"Little by little, ... Little by little ..." the tune jerked along. She liked the smooth one they played next a lot. "One more time, ... just one more time." The singer pleaded in a deep hoarse voice, "You can bawl me out, you can call me names if you'll only let me play those parlor games one ... more ... time." That one tickled her. He sounded so desperate, yet comical too. She tapped her hand on a bolt of cloth on the counter and even felt she could dance to that piece. "One... more ... time." Her new shoes almost got her going to that tune.

Roy saw her, arms lifted slightly from her sides, taking little disjointed steps to the music. He watched for a while, giving his head a shake from time to time, till the record stopped. When he came to ask her if she needed any help, she said not yet, she had to look first, and that reminded her to look up at the shelves again. Pa had told her to pick out anything she liked for Miss Simpson to sew up for her. It made her feel shaky sometimes the way Pa would tell her to do all these things on her own, but she guessed if she could get shoes she could pick out material if she tried.

Then she saw it, way up high, just a narrow strip of color but that was the one she wanted. She didn't have to worry about making up her mind at all, because that was the one.

She asked Roy if she could please see that pink one and he gave his narrow ladder that ran on a track a push that sent it to the right place and he skipped up to the bolt and down with it in no time at all and spread a length of it out on the counter. She could feel the color come over her. It was like spring sunlight with peach blossoms drifting in it.

"Peach voile," Roy said.

She told Roy right away she would like enough of that for a dress, and he asked "long sleeves or short." and when she took a little time wondering about that, he said, "why don't we just make it enough for either, and you can talk it over with Miss Simpson." He snipped across the piece with short blunt scissors and took it over to where he could match it up with thread himself and wrapped it up and wrote it down in the little book that was specially for what she and Pa bought, all so quick she could hardly remember seeing him do it.

Going out of the store with her package, it was as if the new shoes hardly skimmed the ground, she felt so light, almost giddy.

When she got back to where Brownie was tethered, Reverend Harper was up on the bandstand tacking up fresh bunting around the platform. She hoped she could get by him without his thinking up anything new, but he saw her, and carefully spit his mouthful of tacks into his hand and said he hoped she would give consideration to what he had told her.

She was so busy thinking about her dress, it took her a moment to remember what he'd said, then she said yes she certainly would, and she would ask Pa. Then, though she thought he was the most unlikely person in the world to tell first, she couldn't help telling someone.

"I'm going to have a peach voile dress to get married in." Her pale eyes shone quietly as a clear dawn, and her smile was radiant. Mr. Harper raised his hat automatically, though not quite sure why, and a little awkwardly because his regular hand for this was full of tacks.

Chapter 12

Everybody counted on the Fourth of July to be the last spree and holiday before the hectic work of the pear season to come. Charlie woke up grudgingly with the realization that there wasn't going to be any sleeping-in for him. He had neglected to drop off the slips for his last load and would have to run down to the shed to do it. Somebody might go telling Hinkley he was careless, otherwise, and he didn't want the old buzzard to have any real grounds for complaint. When Vivian stirred in the bed he told her he would be back to take her and the kids to the parade, and unshaven, unbreakfasted, he hauled himself up heavily into the truck and mashed the starter till the motor caught. He took the road through the low brush on the mesa fast, his mouth and eyes grim, and jammed on the brakes hard when he got to the bridge into town.

The bridge, steel, instead of the old wooden one, had been called "the new bridge" for decades. It took off at right angles where the road narrowed to skirt the hill that turned the creek north. It couldn't possibly have been laid out worse, Charlie reflected. Like the square turns and T-crossings in the big valley, it regularly caused minor accidents. The bridge landed on Main Street, pointing straight at the middle of Konocti. Though the mountain appeared to sit squarely at the end of the street, it had the faint lavender cast of distance.

He was sore at Mt. Konocti. It had laid down the lava and ash that made the valley fertile, of course, but it hadn't put down enough, and it must have skipped his place, pardon me, the Hinkley place, entirely.

For a block or two, low wooden houses edged Main Street, shaded by oaks and walnut trees that had grown to dwarf them. Charlie scanned the long block of closed shops and stores. They offered nothing, certainly not the hot coffee he needed. When he passed the garage at its end be remembered when he was a kid, watching Glen Crowell the day he first got a job driving for Shell Oil. Buoyant and tall, he had swung up into the high seat of the big red and yellow truck as though he was conquering a spirited horse. Charlie had been fired with ambition to become such a figure.

Across the street the small brick hotel with its green fringe of lacy black-locust foliage showed no life, but then, it seldom did. It was a big comedown from the ornate showplace built in the old days for traveling salesmen and vacationers on their way to the tonic hot springs that bubbled and stank in the hills. That one had burned down, leaving only a piece of its wide veranda with white railings that now graced a squat cottage set in the big space. Empty lots deep in pale shaky wild oats with a scatter of golden poppies stretched beyond to a sagging gray plank building with its windows boarded up, the town's defunct funeral parlor. Charlie remembered when he and Viv crawled into it through the broken windows at dusk, hunting for a place to neck while her parents finished shopping. Inside, apothecary cabinets with small drawers sifted chemical stuff from glass vials onto the dust caking the floor.

On the south side, where Main Street became a country road again, stood a small white Catholic church with a steeple, doors padlocked, he knew, except for Sundays and funerals. The Catholics had got scarcer since the early days. Beyond it where the road split to wrap the foot of the mountain, he turned left, where orchards stretched toward the lake. A couple of minutes to run through the entire town.

The worst part was, in spite of the discontent sickening his belly, the quiet street, fresh with morning, still seemed to breathe a nameless promise. As soon as he drove through the gate into the yard of the packing house he could see Giorgio's red Olds parked alongside the box shed. He kept the truck close to the fence on the opposite side of the lot, and drew up in back of the weatherboard office shack, feeling fully ridiculous to be sneaking around like a kid, and in a decrepit ten ton truck, at that. He took the delinquent load slip over to the drop slot under the office window and pushed it in carefully. Then he saw Gloria standing beside the desk inside, watching him.

She opened the door, saying "Hello, Handsome, come on in." Charlie had to smile at that, remembering. She had called him "Handsome" back when she didn't seem like anything to him, but a grubby little kid, who liked to pretend she was on the make for him when he didn't think she actually knew what she was talking about. The compliment flowed over him like sunshine.

He started to explain about the slip. She took it and put it on one of the piles arranged on the desk. "Don't worry about it, I'll fix it. I'm just setting up some files for the season." Gloria was the daughter of one of the members of the Growers Association. She used to help in the office when they got snowed under. She still did, keeping it up to date with what she learned in her job in Hopland.

If Gloria knew she had been the town scandal when she had run off with a fruit tramp, she never showed it. She and Giorgio turned up exactly at the right time before the pears were ready, and went to work as usual. That was five years ago. When the fruit was rolling in fast she could make almost as much packing pears, with overtime, as Giorgio did making boxes, so they had plenty to spend. They had been to Honolulu and Mexico, which wasn't like real tramps, who usually didn't have enough money to get back to where they came from, even.

She sure didn't look like a local girl any more. She had on a short tight skirt, and a row of bracelets up her bare arm. The short hair puffed out curly over her ears was an ordinary medium brown, not what you might expect with the olive tone of her skin. Under the calm curves of her eyebrows, her gray eyes were level and steady, a faint challenge in them contradicting her serene look. Shiny red lipstick went all the way out to the corners of her mouth. All told, it was quite a combination.

She surveyed him, smiling. "I see you got your health back," she said. Charlie rubbed the stubble on his cheek, suddenly feeling as self-conscious as a kid.

"Pretty much," he agreed. He and Gloria had been the best team of clowns in the whole school. After all the gags they had pulled together, the hours of laughing and scheming they had spent then, he couldn't think of a word to say to her now. She waited to see what Charlie would do, the way everybody used to. Giorgio's hammer, at the far end of the shed yard, rang clear and silvery, making the wide space around the shed seem especially empty and quiet, like a Sunday morning.

By ten o'clock it was hot. People were pulling into town for the parade from all directions. Bob Dermot kept his barber shop open so farmers who lived far out could spruce up; the Tallmans were ready with extra cakes and pies lining the shelves behind the counter, and a block of ice in the extra ice box out back. The drugstore was open for emergencies. Front porches along the street were set with chairs, and benches had been planted wherever there were shade trees.

The parade was assembling under the big walnut trees on Jimmy Gunn's place, almost at the foot of the bridge on the town side to the north. It was in a hubbub. The high school band, the Queen of the Fourth and actors on the various floats that retold Lake County's seventy-five years of history, and one commemorating its existence before that as an Indian paradise, were all arguing about whether the historic sequence should start with the olden times, or begin with the present and run backward, and whereabouts in it the Queen should appear. Queen first, they finally decided, to be followed by the band, with history dwindling backwards.

Beth was one of the señoritas on the Spanish Days display, with a tall comb bobby-pinned upright in her black hair and a black lace mantilla to flirt through. Although they figured Kelsey was the first really white man in the county, the first rancher of all had been Salvatore Vallejo, Colonel in the Mexican army, who had a huge land grant on which he had run cattle. Quite a few of the women in town liked to dress up as señoritas, so the Spanish Days float was loaded, with Vallejo riding one of the horses in the team that pulled it, and his foot soldiers marching behind.

Kelsey got a kind of tribute as founder. Myrna Kelsey, his last descendant, was Miss Lake County Bartlett, and rode in a leafy bower in the back of a pick-up truck, representing the pear industry, presently foremost in the county. Myrna felt the town owed it to her ancestor, who, for better or worse, provided Lake County the event that got it into history books at all, and he had suffered a lot of criticism for it lately. Because of the way he treated the Indians, they had murdered him one night, and a few months later U.S. Government troops had retaliated, attacking the Indian village and killing more than a hundred of its inhabitants, men, women, and children. Myrna could thank Daniel Colson for digging up that story. He had started researching the county's history when he broke his back and couldn't work, and had come across documentation for it in the town's own library. Of all he things he had written, that piece was the one that had got published. Daniel Colson, the neighbors agreed, was a born troublemaker, and she shouldn't pay it any mind. Anyway, she enjoyed her prominence and having a shady place to sit while they waited for the parade to begin.

Myrna was dressed in a yellow sateen gown puffed out somewhat bumpily with crumpled tissue paper, so that she crackled softly when she moved. In her lap she held a flat gold pan with a handful of dried Lake County pears in the bottom for the nuggets. Walnuts and prunes, less important in the economy, were played by very small children in tan and purple crepe paper costumes riding in a bed of straw on the floor. Their mothers were hanging about the truck trying to keep them from tearing the costumes, chatting with Myrna, and playing the delicate game of being cordial to Helena Hotchkiss, the Queen, without quite including her on an equal footing.

Helena was a niece of one of the County Supervisors, which everybody supposed was how she had got the honor. She was a comely, modest looking girl, and one of the few who could ride a horse, which was always good in a parade.

But she did have a strapping eight-month old son and no husband to show for it, and while they didn't want to be vindictive, still, most of them felt, there should be a distinction made.

Beth watched this byplay soberly, through her drooping mantilla. She would have liked to be the official queen of the parade, whether Bill thought the whole thing was ridiculous or not, instead of just the prettiest girl in it, which she knew she was.

She watched Helena with a sidelong fascination, while the horse paced and wheeled, and Helena bent forward to pat its neck contentedly as though she never had a thought in the world about whether she was a disgrace or not. Helena had been the first girl to stay right there in town while she got bigger in the sight of all and had her baby there. Her whole family was proud of the strong child and paraded it as if it were the most natural thing in the world. Helena was wearing a cowboy hat and chaps, though these didn't have anything to do with Lake County history, they made her look a lot more dashing than she ordinarily did. Beth appraised her: on a horse she had style.

Getting the band lined up to follow the Queen was holding up the whole assemblage. Mr. Boyden, who was the high school science, mathematics and band teacher, arranged the eleven wind instruments, piccolo first. Though shy, they were pleased to be performing, but mainly they were noisy and eluded Mr. Boyden's grouping. Mr. Nelson, the school janitor who played many instruments in his lonely time off and had taught almost everyone in the section, was standing by to help the boys tune up. The sound went tootling and squalling about for a long time while he shook his head and protested and insisted. Finally satisfied, he nodded at them all, beaming, and said, "Now that is tune."

The last player, not strictly part of the KUHS band at all, was a calm, stocky child recruited desperately from grammar school fourth grade when the band's drummer failed to show up. He stood ready and at ease behind his bass drum which was propped securely in a red toy wagon to be pulled ahead by his still smaller brother.

Vallejo had a little trouble swinging his team in behind Miss Bartlett Pear's float; but as soon as he managed it, the Indians who were real Indians, gunned their truck into place. They had a teepee and a fake campfire on the truck bed, and were smoking long peace pipes. One woman who still knew how to do it was weaving a reed basket. After them, anybody who wanted to could join the parade and carry a flag if they had one. Mr. Boyden was tapping his baton for the band's attention, without getting any. In the midst of the confusion, the small drummer boy watched and listened. Then, as if sensing the moment had come if it was ever going to, he raised his round padded drum stick higher than his head, and launched on the air a sequence of beats so exultant and compelling that the band started to attention, Mr. Boyden caught the rhythm with his baton, and presently they were all playing as never before. The whole parade, which had looked unready, moved forward into line and curved off toward Main Street. Mr. Nelson smiled and nodded recognition of the truth and power of the beat.

Charlie, with a truckload of neighbor kids hanging over the bottom half of the side rails, and Vivian holding on to the door, heard the first drum beats as the truck crossed the bridge. From its height, he could see the parade wheeling out of Gunn's driveway and climbing the slight rise to Main Street. Charlie sailed down the cleared street, near the corner. Beulah, with Jess in front of the barber shop, was pleased when she saw this. She always felt like she was going to have a good time when she saw Charlie.

"You nut," Viv said, holding on as they jolted to a stop, though she liked the view from the high seat. She grinned at Charlie as she said it, and pulled the wide brim of her straw hat down on either side of her face as she scanned the street intently. The head of the parade was just barely in sight at the end of the street, but the drum made her feel like something terrific was about to happen.

There was not supposed to be any parking on Main Street during the parade. Charlie smiled as he thought up some spurious logic to confuse Harv, who was sort of town constable, if he challenged Charlie's position. The kids lined up on the street side with their elbows hung over the top of the guard rails, and Robbie accommodated himself to looking between them. When he turned to Charlie to ask him when the parade was going to start, Charlie turned a pear lug over for him to stand on, and asked, "Can you see it?"

"I can see a horse," he said.

"Fine," Charlie said. Viv glanced at them. Charlie saw that her face was flushed, and her eyes were shooting out blue sparks. It made you want to look around and find out what was so exciting. She had on a yellow dress that looked good even though it showed her waist was getting thicker. He'd gotten pretty used to thinking of Viv in an apron. A kind of gloom seemed to be descending out of the sky onto him, but it hadn't dimmed Viv or the kids. A one-man cloud, he thought, just for me.

At the far end of the street, Helena lowered her eyes with a modest, even disparaging glance at her hands which held the reins perfectly, guiding her shining mount in a stately pace down Main Street. Some of the parade watchers knew in advance that Helena was going to be Queen, some did not, but they all knew about the illegitimate boy whose father she refused to identify.

Helena's uncle the supervisor, had a whole lot of say in the town. It was hard for those who wanted to be thoughtful about their behavior to know where to turn. Anyway, since she was heading the parade, they hadn't much option open but to look up and applaud. A few of the women turned to each other in delicious aristocracy of disapproval when they recognized the unwed Queen, but most went on clapping with a bland unfocused look.

As Helena drew alongside Beulah's shady spot, Beulah turned to Jess and said, "Isn't that a pretty color for a horse, though, Jess." She remembered hearing that Helena had a baby, a son, and that it had no father. It was funny that they would say that, she thought. Everything that got born had a father of some kind. Her baby's father was Jess, she knew that, or would be when it came. She folded her arms gently across her belly, and smiled out at the flag rippling silkily, the uplifted trumpets flashing as the band stepped along, and the dappled sun on the road shifting delicately with the breeze. She could hardly contain her pleasure.

It hit Charlie right in the stomach when he realized Helena was Queen of the day. He turned to Viv, "That's a hell of an example for the kids isn't it," he said scornfully. That fancy cowboy hat might just as well have been a crown. The Hotchkisses had put a good face on it, and he supposed that was all right, you had to stick by your family, but that kid was still a bastard, and someday they were going to run up hard against that fact, and it wouldn't call for any celebration. It was fine to be broad-minded and all, but a bastard was no joke.

Since Beth's Spanish Days float was next to last, she could watch the others up close as they turned the corner onto Main Street and really began to hit their stride. She caught Helena's pride in her horsemanship and her crown. "I should learn to ride a horse," she thought irritably. Helena had a lot of nerve. Or rather, she had a lot of relatives. There sure wasn't any political pull in the Hafner family to make a place in the sun for an illegitimate kid if she had one. All the same, Helena had a lot of guts, you had to honor that.

There went Myrna Kelsey, actually rosy-cheeked above that ghastly yellow sateen. And she looked proud, well anyway, smug, as though that ancestor of hers had been anything but a disgrace to humanity. This was some parade, she thought. As her float rounded the corner and started down the street she swung her right hip out a little, and folded the mantilla back from her face.

Bill and Irv watched from the sidewalk in front of Tallman's until Beth's float had gone by. Bill turned away to go in for a coke, and waited for Irv at the door.

"Where are you going?" he asked him when Irv started walking away.

"I'm going to get Beth."

"They'll all come back as soon as they're done," Bill said. Irv turned away sharply and started down the walk, head down. Bill let Tallman's screen door fall closed and started after him, slowly, as though the matter required thought. They both trudged along the sidewalk, about twenty feet apart. When the walk ended, Bill overtook Irv in the path by the road, and they kicked along through the dust together side by side.

There was a turnaround for cars in the yard back of the Catholic church. The parade floats nosed into the edge of the circle as they finished up the parade. "Looks like we're expecting hostile Indians," General Vallejo said.

"Well here they come," Queen Helena said, as the last of the displays, the truck with the batch of Pomo and their teepee crawled into the driveway. Helena was still flushed with triumph. All the women looked excited and glowing as they climbed off the trucks, not anxious to give up their fancy roles.

Beth jumped down breathless into the extended arms of the driver of the Spanish Days float who had been planning this maneuver for several blocks. Beth had seen Bill and Irv waiting by the church and wondered how they managed to beat the parade there when she had seen them in front of Tallman's and Bill, at least looked like he was heading in for a drink. She had counted on Irv to show up for her, but figured Bill might decide it wasn't reasonable to come way out to the church since she had to come back to town anyway. The heavy points of hair swung across her cheeks as she sauntered toward the two men. Her eyes were shining as she neared them, dropping her eyelids and raising them slowly for a full sweep of lashes, and batting them again. It was because of Irv she could clown it up. There he was just standing quietly; his blue gaze telling her that she was beautiful. Bill had tossed his head back, as she came close, too. That was Bill's way, not telling her anything if he could help it. She didn't feel like sparring, maybe because for once she felt she couldn't lose, or maybe because she couldn't bear it if she did, after feeling so good. She just wanted to hook arms and stroll back to town for a coke.

Irv moved toward her just then, offering his arm. He didn't know why he thought she needed it. She looked like she never needed help, less with excitement like a strong wind in her sails. Bill joined them, leisurely. "¿Quiere usted una Coca Cola, Señorita?" he asked.

Tallman's was crowded: tables were full and people were standing several deep around the counter. Drinks and money were passed back and forth overhead, and people popped their own bottle tops to drink where they stood, chatting as though it were a big party. Most of the crowd were men, picking up cold sodas for the family while the women spread out picnic lunches on tables under trees down by the creek or on the porches on Main Street.

All around her Beth could feel the admiration of the men, as plainly as if they lifted her on their shoulders and toasted to her. Bill felt it too, and had a brief impulse to show that she was his girl, though that was exactly what he had been careful not to do. He actually felt a twinge of envy himself when he had watched Beth hook arms to walk back to town with Irv. It was so peaceful, as though she had lost interest in the affect she made. He'd never seen her do that before. He'd never seen Irv like this either.

Irv and he often had had crushes on the same girl when they were kids in Oakland. It was assumed Bill would be favored over Irv, but it had always been all right. It was like the dozens of wrestling matches they had, which Irv always won. They went on wrestling as serenely as they collected stamps or played Black Jack together. This was different, Irv was so serious. But what in God's name was he thinking of? He wasn't thinking at all, of course.

After lunch the heat began to accumulate sullenly. It glared down from the sky and reflected back from sidewalks and buildings. Porch parties retreated inside houses, and a lot of people left for the lake after the parade.

Down at the picnic ground beside the creek grownups snoozed in the shade while children splashed in the water or played on the tilted precarious remains of the hanging bridge that still spanned a narrow place. The bridge, of slats, wire and rope, had been sturdy enough to survive for years until the floods a few seasons ago wrecked it. Grim little nosegays of twigs and debris caught far up in the support cables showed how high the water had come.

Jimmy Gunn, who was the mechanical whiz in school, was speculating about the rusting remains of an old Stanley Steamer marooned in the creek bed north of the bridge. Sand had sifted all over it, and it was rusted brown, but Jimmy insisted the works were so simple they were still good: there wasn't anything to break. Clean it up and fire the boiler and it might even run. "Why don't we," Lester said. Jimmy's flivver was quickly filled with recruits, ready to go.

"Can we come?" Jeanne asked. She and Izzy were bored playing with the little kids.

"If you carry water." Jimmy said.

The bank towered over the resting place of the old steamer, and gave them shade as half the crew labored to fill up the boiler and the other half scouted for wood. Jimmy and Lester worked on the car, chipping and scraping away the rust with wire brushes and kerosene, jiggling any parts that would jiggle, conferring amiably as they had for years together, quiet voiced, conversationally.

The water carriers were happy in the wet and the shadows. The woodmen came back puffing and boiling with the heat streaming from the brilliant sapphire sky and glaring back from the stones and gravel of the creek bed. Jimmy insisted that if they were going to get anywhere they would need wood with some real heat in it, not that pulpy stuff the sun and water had leached out, and sent them forth again. Finally satisfied, he built a fire on the stones under the boiler. He was planning his moves for when the steam was up when he noticed someone on the bank high above them waving his arms and hollering something he couldn't make out. A slow weakness of his movements convinced Jimmy it was a real emergency. He and Lester abandoned the steamer seat and took off with the flivver.

Lester came back on foot to tell the others what happened. There was some trouble. Jimmy had to drive the guy in to get an ambulance, somebody was hurt, or sick. He didn't know what was the matter, but the guy acted like it was serious and was about to collapse, himself. Lester said if they had to get an ambulance in this county on a holiday it might take all day, so the troupe started to trudge back along the creek. Beyond the shade of the bank the heat hit them like a bludgeon. One of the small boys pretended to have a heart attack in hope of being carried. The little ones flopped into every deep spot the creek offered.

Viv and Charlie broke off talking to listen to Iz and Jeanne's story when they got back, but they didn't get excited about it—it was as if they knew already. Charlie even got up and went down to the creek and started tossing pebbles into it, with his back turned. It seemed quieter in the grounds than it ought to be, too. Several parties were packing up to leave.

"What's the matter, Mama," Izzy asked Vivian. "It seems like Papa's acting funny, and won't even say why."

"Never mind," Vivian said. "You and Jeanne go round up everybody we brought and tell them to get ready to leave. It's time we went home."

Izzy looked at her a minute, trying to figure out what was going on. Were they having a fight? It didn't quite seem like that was it. She said alright, she would get the little ones out of the water and dried, then. Jeanne said she'd go into town and gather up any who might be hanging around Tallman's.

After Jeanne returned with the strays she complained to Isobel, "Never mind, never mind, that's all anybody will say. I don't think they know anything extra anyway. They're just acting queer, even Bill." She was silent for a while after this acknowledgement. It was the sore point—Bill usually told her things. "I listened beside the Baer's screen porch on the way back. A bunch of women were talking all hushed and huddled together like they were telling ghost stories. I heard one saying something about a Doberman that had clawed his way right through a screen door, and a little poodle lying dead in a pool of blood, but what's eating everybody isn't about dogs."

She caught sight of Ben, the last Rincon child still missing from Charlie's truckload, and ran after him till she caught him.

"Gee, why do we have to leave now when it's just getting fun," he complained, pulling back stubbornly to test Jeanne's grip.

She hauled him to the box set by the tailgate so the kids could climb into the back of the truck. "Never mind," she snapped. "Just get in."

After the young ones were in bed for the night, Viv asked Charlie just what happened anyway. She had the feeling she was being treated like another one of the kids. "What went on? And who was it," she persisted. "What's this hush-hush atmosphere all about, Charlie? Do you know?"

Charlie looked down at the table, "Actually I don't. And I don't know who it was either. About the only one we could figure was missing from here was Helena, our Queen."

He wished he didn't have to go on. He felt almost like Viv, that something dark and dangerous was being kept secret from him, but he also felt like a perpetrator, as though there were two sides to be on, and he had somehow wound up on the bad side—the side of the secret-hiders. What he had to hide was Gloria—not that he had done anything, God knows, but he had a kind of objective feeling, as though it was out of his hands, that he was going to. As if that wasn't enough, it seemed like the shock and revulsion that was in the air now about the accident in the creek bed was getting linked up in his mind with Gloria and him. That was weird, but he couldn't shake it off.

He had to go on—Viv was watching him. "All I know is what Douglas said. They checked with him to see if he had some stuff on hand in the pharmacy that they needed at the hospital. He said he didn't know who was involved either. Then Frank Hafner and Earl Green came into the store too, with Frank all steamed up to pull some vigilante stuff to protect womankind, except he didn't know what from. It was a mess, everybody arguing without knowing what they were talking about. Douglas finally told Frank that if he or anyone else wanted to fight about something they didn't know anything about, would they please leave the drugstore. He refused to be party to it."

Chapter 13

Jeanne had been hearing about cutting pears for almost a year, from Izzy, and others too, and it still wasn't clear exactly why first you only scooped out the brittle star at their blossom ends and stacked them in a pan, or how you pulled the stems off with one knife sweep as you cut them in half.

"It's easy, you'll see." everybody assured her. They also said, "Of course they'll hire you, you live in the gulch."

The one thing she was sure of was what she was going to buy with the money she earned: the pair of imitation snake skin trimmed oxfords in the Sears Roebuck catalog and the ivory paralyn dresser set, and especially the white beret and bell bottom jeans like Izzy's.

She was glad when the call came to start work, whether or not she knew what she was supposed to do. She took her new knife and corer and two big flat-bottomed pans and her oilcloth apron with an orange poppies design. Bill dropped her off at the shed, where the wives of the neighborhood, and their young ones not yet adept enough to work at the packing sheds were already choosing the tables and partners they wanted. Some of the mothers had brought smaller children, too, who stood on overturned lugs, aproned from chin to toes, and cut out the blossom ends or fussed with the scars and worm tracks that would slow their mothers down, otherwise.

Katherine Meyer's shoulders, two tables in front of hers, swung like oiled machinery as she paved tray after tray with glistening pear halves so fast you could almost see the rows marching down their lengths. She noticed Katherine would holler, "Box!" when the bottom of the one she had was covered, so the boy would get there with a fresh box while she still had a heaped-up panful to halve. She didn't lose a stroke between boxes. Her ticket was attached to the shoulder straps of her apron where they were tied together so they couldn't fall down over her arms and hold her back. It stuck out from her body, quivering with her movements. The box boy would catch it and punch out the next number without her having to look up.

Izzy, working at the table next to hers, looked kind of resigned and steady from the back. She had cut pears for four seasons already, and was pretty good at it, just not grim and mechanical like Katherine.

Most everybody seemed like they were having a good time, though. They had little jokes from the years before that Jeanne did-n't understand yet. The older women looked like they enjoyed sitting on a box to wait a minute if the fruit or a fresh tray was slow coming. Usually there was some talk or laughing going on somewhere.

The men stacked fresh redwood shake trays on top of the filled ones, four or five or more high at the tables, whatever was comfortable for the cutters, When they got too high the cutter would call "Trays away," and the tray men would come and shift the whole stack one by one onto a car that ran on a narrow gage track beside the tables. They rinsed the fruit off with a sprinkler hose, and then pushed the stacked car out to the sulfur shed, where pots of yellow sulfur were lit to smoke overnight to bleach the fruit and kill any bugs or worm eggs before the trays were laid in the sun to dry. The field at the back where they were spread was hedged round with low chemise. The blue sky came right down to its edges like a lid. It was funny how this spot in the brush seemed like it was a whole busy world during pear season, when the rest of the time you rode right past it as if it wasn't there at all.

You could hear trucks coming up to the front occasionally, and the men deciding where the new fruit should be stacked depending on how ripe it was, and when everybody happened to be quiet at once you could hear a bee or yellow jacket buzzing around the pans. The dollars of light that fell on the redwood trays from tiny holes in the roof, stretched out to long ovals as the afternoon went on.

Jeannie's tray partner was a plump girl about two years older than her. She plunked the pears down methodically on her side of the table moving slowly, but still on every tray she had to bring her pan over to Jeannie's side and help her fill it before they yelled for another. She was cheerful and nice about it, so Jeannie felt guilty for hating to watch her pull up the straps of her slip that kept sliding down her fat arms with her hooked corer that was all dirty with pear goo. She wished she could have Izzy for a partner, but everybody said partners should be about the same speed, or it wasn't fair.

The shed boss came through showing a new boy the ropes. Jeanne saw that the new boy was watching Izzy every chance he got. She thought he was pretty good looking, mainly because he was tall, and moved in a way that was sort of grand, though he didn't look conceited. His light brown hair rose away from his face in a cowlick, almost like a wave, and he had a kind of peaceful smile, that showed how even and straight his teeth were, white too, and when the boss left, he came over to Isobel's tray and looked up under the fall of fluffy gold hair around her face. Izzy looked up, laughing with surprise, and as she answered his question about the pears, blushed. Jeannie was close enough to see it made her look pretty.

He kept asking Izzy stuff about the shed, and it sounded like he was really interested in it, but he also didn't pretend he wasn't interested in Izzy, too. She talked more than she usually did, because of the questions. She told him how almost everybody knew each other in the shed because they lived in the same branch valley, the Rincon. They called it the "gulch" in fun. He sorted through the box of pears she was working on, lifting misshapen and wormy ones up, and wrinkling his nose. Izzy said, well, sure, the pears they dried were mostly culls of one sort or another. Now they had refrigerator cars, the fancy fruit was all packed and shipped green, where before it had all been dried. The packing sheds was where the money was now, the boy said. He knew, he lived with some packers, and it was a pretty tense business. Jeannie was amazed at what all Izzy knew about the pear business.

By the end of the first day she was sick and tired of cutting pears. She had learned all there was to know, except how to do it fast, and it was pretty boring. The space under the big shed roof was filling up with lugs of green pears stacked solid as high as the men could handle them. The box boys always hunted for the ripest fruit to bring to the tables to be cut, leaving meandering narrow aisles and hidden rooms carved out of the blocks of lugs. Jeannie longed to hide out and read a book in one of these cool nooks, but she kept working steadily because everybody else did. She wondered how many boxes Katherine cut in a day. It sure wasn't four, which was what Jeanne's card said she had done. Fifty cents. She supposed she'd get faster than that, but she was sure she wasn't ever going to get passionate about it.

The next morning the boy showed up for work as a box boy and some new women fruit tramps came in to work at the empty tables that stretched way out under the shade of the long shed. He was assigned to the newly opened section at first, but after a couple of days, he was up front, serving boxes to Izzy and Jeanne, and the other locals. He spent his time between calls for boxes talking to Izzy whenever he could.

Usually the crew could just about keep up with the fruit, but it ripened according to its own time table, and sometimes as the season peaked, part of the crew had to work overtime to save it from rotting. One afternoon, though there were still plenty of fruit left, none was ripe enough to cut. The box boy got up on top to see if they could spot any islands of ripe fruit, but reported nothing but green everywhere. They would have to knock off for a day or so.

The women took advantage of the early closing to wash their pans and knives better than usual, the men sat down for a smoke before they pushed the last trays into the sulfur shed. Katherine managed to get the last ripe box set up at her table and was going through it like a buzz saw, looking madder than ever.

Nobody else seemed in a hurry to leave. They sat on upended boxes and even ate a few of the last ripe pears. Jeanne got a ride to the swimming hole, counting on Bill to stop by and take her home. Izzy who lived almost directly down hill from the shed said she would walk home.

The flivvers and trucks raised the dust as they passed Izzy on the shed road. She fanned it away from her face laughing and shook her head when anyone yelled, "Want a ride?" When she got to the narrow road winding down from the mesa to the Rincon, she heard a motorcycle idling behind her, and turned to look back.

Kenny, the new box boy, promptly rode up beside her. "I didn't want to scare you," he said balancing the bike with one foot down on the road. "Would you like a ride?"

"Oh, yes!" Izzy said. Then she started to qualify—it wasn't far home, she didn't mind walking.

"Get up back of me, we'll take a spin into town for a soda first. O.K?"

"Won't it tip if I do? "

"Don't worry, we're used to it."

She hardly knew which scared her most, the bike or getting up so close to the good-looking outsider, but she was going to do it if it killed her. She climbed up behind him while he braced both legs. "Hold onto my waist and don't do anything, just go along with me."

She had put her hands politely on his sides, but as they wound down the hill to the bottom land, even though he was going slow, she had to circle his waist to keep from swinging off. When he began to streak along the road by the creek, he yelled back, "Put your head down on my back if the wind bothers you," and she did what he told her to do, as though she was taking a lesson, but she held back from pressing her breasts against him. Her heart was beating too fast and she felt confused.

When he slowed down to tell her he was going to zigzag, and that she should just sort of sway with him, she got so she could. It was like following a good dancer.

After a while she raised her head up so she could get the wind in her hair and watch the trees streaming by. When they hit a bumpy stretch, she tightened her arms around Kenny's waist with more confidence because she felt she knew what she was doing, sort of.

They didn't ford the creek where cars did, but went upstream a ways where the banks were steep but the water was more shallow. They hit the water pretty fast, and made a high-sided trough as they went through it, then they surged up the far bank like an animal taking a good run at the start and just barely managing to struggle over the top. Kenny swept the bike to a stop and stood spraddled, looking back at Izzy.

"Did you like that?" he asked, when he could tell by her face she loved it.

She was laughing at how wobbly she felt, and catching her breath. "It was wonderful! Did you know we could make it up the bank like that?"

"Oh, sure. A bike can do a lot if it wants to. Someday you can sit in front of me and steer, if you want." She thought how proud and elegant he looked drawing off his leather gloves and stuffing them in his jacket pockets.

Mr. Tallman's sodas were frothy and thick with ice cream and strawberries. They sat at the counter looking at each other over their straws in the mirror. Both their faces were flushed with the heat, and their smiles were funny around the straws, as though they couldn't help smiling even though it stopped the straw action. Kenny's head was higher in the mirror, because he was tall, and his hair and eyes were darker than hers and his face more tanned. She looked little and pale in the mirror, she thought. The only thing you could really tell was that her eyes were blue. For a minute Izzy got flustered and looked down, watching her soda disappear by sips, but she was too exhilarated for that, and looked up again, laughing. Kenny was still watching her with the same smile.

The big Indian was parked by the tethering post in front of the bandstand. They mounted it like old hands, and struck a sedate pace down main street and across the bridge, where Kenny gunned it a bit so the sharp corner south would provide a little sport. As soon as they sped up Izzy pressed close to him and laid her cheek against the broad shield of his back. It was as though she leaned against a glowing light that went right through her body and lit it up too. She felt that anybody who passed them couldn't help but know what was happening in her, but she wasn't going to stop because of that or anything else. She pressed closer. When they turned onto the mesa road, cut through high brush, its silty red dust felt soft under the wheels. Kenny slowed down to use it rather than fight it, and for a while they drifted through an endlessly parting gray-green sea trailed by the swirling red dust cloud. She reached her arms farther around his waist, lightly, to hold more of him. The sun was getting into some thin clouds as it lowered, tinting the sunshine with red. Izzy watched their shadow ripple along with them against the hedge of brush. She didn't want this feeling to ever stop, though now wherever their bodies touched it was sharp as a cry. Kenny slowed as much as the machine could handle, as though he was listening, and feeling the same way. The warm smell of sage in the chemise, and the sweetness of manzanita blossoms came in drifts. She couldn't hear anything but the roar of the motor, but the pounding of her heart was so strong, she felt like they could hear that too.

All at once a cloud of dust churned up right around them, choking them and almost blinding them, and the angry clatter of a truck going too fast for the road climbed above their roar. By the time she turned her head to the other side there was nothing in sight but a veil of dust hanging around the next curve.

The brush began to thin out, and after they took the left turn that headed them back toward the creek, Izzy recognized the very spot Kenny had stopped to pick her up. It seemed like that had been a long time ago.

They turned south at the bottom this time, and she pointed to show Kenny where to turn in to her place. He braced the bike with both legs and held her arm as she got off. They heard the barn door slam, and Charlie was coming toward them, his arms loaded with provisions from town. He stood glaring. His face turned a dark brick color under his tan, while his lips thinned down tight.

"This is Kenny, Pa," Izzy said, in a small pinched voice, and she almost stumbled as she took a step away from him, as though the earth was shifting under her. She had never seen Pa look so awful, and she couldn't bear to have him say anything mean about Ken.

"Kenny, huh," was what he said, but it was as though he had spit. He bent his head down and started to the house with his load. Izzy could see that his steps were still uneven from his hurt back, and that he held himself with one shoulder twisted up a little as if to ward off something.

She turned to look at Kenny, whose long legs poised on either side of the Indian looked ready to go. She couldn't do a thing except look up at him.

"I'll see you," he said. His voice was husky, but he didn't pay any attention to it. He didn't smile the whole time he looked at her. He took the rutted driveway slowly, but she could hear him on the straightaway going so fast is sounded like the motor was singing.

A potato was still rolling on the floor where it has spilled when Charlie had flung the bags down on the table. Izzy tried to go straight through to her room, but Charlie said, "Come back here. What were you doing with that tramp?"

Her voice had a burst of anguish in it. "He's not a tramp. He gave me a ride home and we went to town for a soda." She turned to get away.

"I thought you had it straight about fruit tramps. If you don't, you better get it now. You're not going to go out with him or any other, ever. If I see you riding hugged up to him again, I'm going to stop you and knock him right off the bike."

Viv ran in from the dining room beyond, and looked at the two in amazement. Izzy was sobbing. "What on earth happened?"

Izzy looked up, beseeching. "Nothing happened, Mama. Kenny gave me a ride home from the shed because we ran out of fruit early." She looked pale and shaking. She stopped crying, but an occasional sob still wracked her.

Viv was looking at Charlie, bewildered. Charlie started out in a tense vindictive voice. "Isobel was snuggled up behind him on a bike..." his voice trailed off.

"Jesus, I don't know," he said. "I just couldn't stand the sight. It seemed like the last straw."

Viv was puzzled. A few days ago he was giving Izzy all that fancy makeup as though he wanted her to blossom out. It was plain crazy. She looked at Charlie in disbelief. He looked black and shut in on himself. She told Izzy, "You better go to your room and calm down. Her voice sounded flat and mean to her own ears, though that wasn't how she felt. Her mind returned to what Charlie said, "It seemed like the last straw," and she felt everything in her head skid to a stop while she wondered what the other straws were. A wave of terror and dread swept over her and a sense of sorrow she couldn't explain.

Chapter 14

Kate Wilkes was ironing out on the screen porch, getting down to the sheets and work clothes at the bottom of her big basket. Sunday school dresses for the girls, on hangers and draped over chairs, already populated the porch. She ironed the work clothes and sheets almost as carefully as the rest. The worn-out parts didn't look so bad when they were ironed smooth. Besides, she had to justify staying out on the porch where it was fresh, and she could see everything happening. Almost as soon as she got started on the jeans, she saw Viv walking in from the main road, swinging along as though she was going somewhere she wanted to go, not looking at all weary and weighed down as she had lately. She bet Viv liked her slippers. She loved Mama's wonderful old stuff, velvet like cream and silk satin so heavy it felt like flesh to touch, but she thought it was too gaudy for a Plain Jane like herself to wear. It had looked like Viv was beginning to feel the same way, which was ridiculous because Viv was beautiful. Even though she didn't gussy herself up or act like a pretty woman any more, she was beautiful. She would like the slippers because they were funny—that sort of gave her leave. When she raised up from unplugging the iron, Viv saw her and waved. Kate went to stand in the door.

Viv bent her head hurrying toward her. She was trying to think of some news or gossip she could deliver to Kate who was always hungry for it. Since Kate didn't drive, and her husband never took her anywhere the extent of her world was just about what she could see from her door: the courtyard and barn with tables for fruit and vegetables strung out under the oak tree, the orchard below the bank reaching toward the cottonwoods at the creek edge, and the truck garden, green and burgeoning in the northern corner by the house. Her husband, Bert, talked little to anyone, including Kate. As far as Viv could see, he just worked hard without comment, scratching a living for his big family. Out of necessity, each of the young ones left the farm as soon as possible, and Kate got a little more wistful with each departure. Viv's stomach tightened as she pictured Stevie heading out on his own like that, hardly more than a youngster.

They settled on the porch with cups of coffee. How've you been, Viv?" Kate ducked her head and peered over the top of her glasses. Viv laughed. Kate liked to parody herself.

Viv looked down a moment, then looked at Kate with a pinched face. "I don't know, Kate. It seems like I'm too busy to notice, much. Fine, I guess." Her eyes, at their deepest blue, were questioning. Kate's pale tired face and sallow gray eyes were gentle as she returned Viv's gaze.

A truck turned into the drive and bounced toward them. "That's Kevin Scott's rig. He comes for vegetables. Do you know him?" Viv shook her head. "He's camped on the Colson place, making wood out of their mush oaks."

"Charlie told me something about an old logger staying on their place," Viv said. "Isn't that Beulah with him?" She followed Kate out to the stand to pick up some berries. Beulah headed toward the two women, and then remembering her new hair-do and her shiny new shoes with buckled straps, ducked her head to watch the stranger's feet under her walk toward them. She said "Good morning, Kate," quite confidently, then to Viv, "Good morning, Mrs. Norton."

Vivian saw her start to hold out her hand, then hesitate, and quickly put forward her own. "My, you look nice, Beulah." Beulah beamed.

Scott was filling a basket with fruits and vegetables at one end of the table where the new-picked produce from the garden was laid out. Viv wondered why Charlie had said "old logger." He was about the same age they were, just different. He was big, and moved deliberately, as though he had made a lot of decisions. Probably what Charlie meant by 'old' was that he used to be a logger and wasn't any more.

"Good morning," he said when the others reached him. He lifted some green beans to show Beulah. "How's this for Blue Lakes, Miss Colson?"

Beulah said she had never seen the like, and Kate told her they were so tender you could just cook them quick and butter them. They didn't need to stew a long time with salt pork at all.

Beulah said, "Well, think of that."

Scott had gathered a few onions, some beets with deeply embossed bronze leaves, rosy radishes, and a stack of yellow apples. "Have you got a new vegetable for me yet, Mrs. Wilkes?"

"Well, not exactly," Kate said, "but I have an idea." She introduced him to Viv, and explained that he was tired of his food. "Mrs. Norton raises rabbits, Mr. Scott. It might help if you teamed your vegetables up with rabbit sometimes."

"I'd be glad to try that." He smiled at Vivian as he made a slight bow to her, and then after a moment, chose the finest Golden Delicious from his basket and extended it toward her.

"What's this?" Viv asked curiously, as she would ask a child who had brought her something.

"An offering," the logger said. "For cooking instructions when I get the rabbit," he added.

Viv took it from his big hand in both of hers. "I'll do my best." she said. She held on to the apple as she looked around for Stevie. He and Beulah were sitting on a wooden bench by the barn. Steve held a piece of newspaper Kate kept at the stand to wrap wet vegetables and was pretending to read a story from it to Beulah. The story was about a boy and a rabbit. Beulah listened, engrossed. Vivian started to say, "Stevie, you can't read any more than Beulah can," but she caught herself in time to change it to, "You can't always get such a such a good audience, can you." She was glad she caught herself, even though she didn't like to cover up like that.

It was three days before Kevin Scott came for the rabbit—early, before the day got hot. Viv let him choose one on the run and grab it by the ears while she held the gunny sack to receive it. She wound the string around the top and tied it quickly. "Do you know how to handle it?" she asked.

"Pretty much. I can deal with a mule-deer."

"You don't have to shoot a rabbit." She said that the meat was like chicken with no fat, and if you browned it in lard, first, then it would make hunter style or fricassee, almost anything.

He leaned over the door of his auto to set the bag down gently on the floor boards where it thumped a couple of times and then quieted. Scott looked about him as he raised up again. "Did you ever think of taking down that dead cottonwood?" he asked her.

"It died so slowly I guess we never thought about it. Kate told me you were doing that out at the Colsons. How do you charge?"

"It depends on how hard a job it is. I do it for the wood, or for part of the wood. I could take that one down quite easily. It could also come down quite easily by itself in a storm."

"I wondered about that the other night when it was groaning in the wind. I'll ask Charlie what he thinks."

He came for another rabbit the next week.

"You're going to get tired of rabbit, too, if you don't pace yourself," Viv said.

"Suppose I cut down the tree, between rabbits. Have you thought about it?"

"Charlie thinks we should do it."

She was coming back from the barn when he arrived with a circular saw mounted on a rack in his truck.

She liked the hollow, clear sound the ax made, and lifted her head from her sewing from time to time to listen to it. Tonk. Tonk. Tonk. Big deliberate strokes. She went out on the back porch to see, lifting Stevie up so he could see too. The logger swung the long handled ax full out, disengaging it and pulling back for the next swing as though it was part of one movement. It was pretty to watch, like a calm diver who knows what he's doing. She went back to the dress she was making for Izzy.

Finally the chopping stopped, and she went out to look. A tall thin fellow she didn't know had joined the logger, and together they were lifting a deep-toothed saw with handles at both ends out of the truck. They walked around the tree, talking, the logger pointing to places on the tree trunk, then tracing a line on the ground, where it would fall, she supposed. Then the two settled into the rhythmic give and take of sawing. She took Stevie inside. Somehow she didn't want to see the tree fall. She imagined how it would keel over slowly, then bounce once a little after the crash, and then settle in ruins. It was dead, of course; still there was a lot of difference from a standing tree and a bunch of torn and broken branches.

Heeeeeooo ook Heeeeeoooo ook. Stevie was wild to see them cut with the circular saw, so they took another trip to the porch. The engine was putt-putting away, tainting the air with blue gasoline-smelling smoke, but the whine of the saw was even and serene, spinning away into the distance, as though you could almost see it travel. It made you realize what a perfect still summer's day it was, between cuts. She almost hated to go back in the house. Stevie kept looking back.

Viv had trouble getting the pleats even in Izzy's skirt, finally having to baste them, to her annoyance. Kate always looked so interested and happy when she was making something, but then Kate sewed like an artist, not just muddling through like she did. Here she was, way over her head with the simplest pattern. She straightened up for a breather.

"Well Stevie, I guess one thing you'll never learn from me is sewing." As she finished saying it, she realized the room was still, Stevie was no longer on the floor tying scraps together for a kite tail, and worse, the saw was no longer singing. She threw the dress off her lap and ran to the kitchen, imagining Stevie running toward the saw, stumbling, falling face forward. She pulled open the door, frantically. From top to bottom it seemed filled with the logger's form, and at the top was Stevie, on his shoulders, riding like a jaunty jockey.

"He admitted he wasn't sure you knew where he was," Scott said. He bent forward in a deep bow so she could lift the child off his neck. Viv took him and held him close, high up, so she could lean her forehead against his as she struggled to get rid of her dizzy feeling and make herself realize she was being foolish! Stevie hadn't been in that kind of danger. Kevin Scott was a trained woodsman, which would include being careful of stray children. She was blowing up the danger and her feeling of being rescued way out of proportion. There was nothing for her to cry over. Telling herself that wasn't changing the way she felt.

Then suddenly Charlie was reaching to take Stevie out of her arms and set him down on his feet. She hadn't heard the truck, and could hardly credit the appearance of Charlie without the clatter of the truck, but there he was. He looked affronted, as though Scott hadn't any business bowing down before his wife, and handing his child over to her. He said crisply that he had forgotten some load slips that were due at the shed, and brushed by Viv into the kitchen so roughly he jostled her. His curt "pardon me" didn't seem to fit the situation.

Chapter 15

Beulah stood in her slip in front of the bird's-eye maple bureau that had been in her room almost as long as she could remember—for years before she was tall enough to look into the mirror above it without pulling a chair over to stand on. She used to do that so she could watch the mirror, and see the trees outside the window in back of her tossing in a wind she couldn't even feel. Now she faced herself in the mirror, and watched closely as Miss Simpson slipped her wedding dress over her head and began to ease it down her body. The peach dress colored in her picture that now filled the mirror like a portrait with leaves all around it sparkling in the sun. She blinked slowly, thinking how pretty it all was. Actually it took some firm two-handed tugs to get the dress on her at all and once it was on, Miss Simpson hastily began to take it off again, saying she would have to make a few little adjustments. The dress that she had basted to fit perfectly a few weeks before now rose alarmingly in front to accommodate what Miss Simpson could only bear to think of as certain changes.

When she and Beulah had gone to Robison's dry goods store together to pick a pattern for the dress, Beulah wanted one of the new formals that had skirts eight to ten inches longer in back than in front. It was graceful and Beulah had the height for it, Miss Simpson thought, but it required presence, which she had not, so she had steered Beulah to a simple pattern with a dropped waist and gathered skirt, which she assured her would look just lovely in the peach voile. The challenge she faced now was to embrace the new fashion that had overtaken them, and to mask Beulah's out-thrust front as much as possible. She kept her composure, as befitted her profession, but she flushed red, so that the gray wart on the bridge of her nose just above the pince-nez stood out more than ever. As she gathered the dress in her arms, and carried it to the table to start her work, her face was averted and her mouth pinched so that vertical lines deepened in her upper lip. Her heart was thumping and she swayed with dizziness, but what she allowed herself to think was that it was a blessing she had got Beulah to order the biggest veil in the Montgomery Ward catalog. It was almost as though she had had a premonition, though at the time all she thought she had to camouflage was Beulah's really almost masculine musculature. At least she had the veil to work with in this emergency.

Beth Hafner arrived to put any last needed touches on Beulah's hairdo. She had picked up Kate Wilkes who had offered to do Beulah's flowers, and now carried a sheaf of lilacs and pink roses from her garden which she laid out on the bed tenderly. She had also brought a wreath of Brewster rose buds and baby breath to crown the veil. Miss Simpson hurried to get the veil on Beulah's head, and Kate stood ready with the wreath while the other fussed with the lace. Beth had unscrewed a light bulb and plugged her curling tongs into the socket, and since the tongs had hissed and sizzled when she tested it with a wet finger, was twirling it in her hand with its jaws open to cool.

The roll of green grosgrain ribbon stuffed with cotton batting protected Beulah's head perfectly from thorns and stems when Miss Simpson slipped the wreath over the veil. The women said it was a sheer work of art. The only problem was finding enough hair to hold the pins. Miss Simpson was thinking "Thank goodness it's tight enough to stay on without them," but Beth tested her iron on a piece of brown paper bag, filling the room with a toasty smell along with the scent of lilacs and roses. A few tight curls in the right place might give the pins something to hold onto, and she wanted to fix a little fluff of bangs to shorten the length of Beulah's face.

Beulah stood smiling, watching a bird on a branch of the tree in the mirror while the women worked.

When Miss Simpson lifted the veil off, she said, very casually, "Why don't you take a little rest while I make the dress alterations, Beulah. It will take me just a few minutes." No need trying it on her again. All she could do was let it out as much as possible.

Beulah thought of the red hen who was due to hatch any day, and murmured there was something in the yard she needed to attend to.

"My dear mother made some alterations in Beulah's mother's clothes, when she and Mr. Colson first came to the county," Miss Simpson said as soon as the door closed after Beulah. She didn't trust Beth's discretion, and wanted to cut off any unseemly comment on Beulah's shape.

"She was a beauty, wasn't she," Kate said. She didn't want the other two to talk about Beulah, either.

"She had a pretty face and form," Miss Simpson conceded.

"Did she really?" Beth asked, looking from one to to another to see if they were fooling. "What did she look like? — Beulah?" She couldn't figure out what these two old girls were doing, pretending Beulah wasn't a freak, and furthermore, a pregnant freak. Even if Ma hadn't tipped her off, she could tell that now, and she wasn't as interested in the subject as the old gossips in town always seemed to be.

Miss Simpson worked intently on the dress in her lap, snipping open seams and stitching them up again quickly as a Kate answered Beth, "She was small and dainty with rich coloring, and perfect little teeth. They came the year after Bert and I did, and I remember her in town, walking down the street on Dan Colson's arm lifting the front of her skirt a bit to keep it out of the dust, and her little parasol set to protect her complexion. She was with child, but she carried the weight all in front and high, and even made her leaned-back walk seem elegant. They made Kelseyville seem like Baltimore. I practiced it all with an umbrella—and Bert, of course."

"She never made the least concession to the change," Miss Simpson said, to put the right light on it.

"How did Colson ever get a wife like that?" Beth asked.

"Daniel Colson was as cultured as she was, or thought she was, and as handsome, even though he was—older." More my age actually, she thought.

"Yeah, I can see how he'd be good looking, if he was headed all in one direction." Beth admitted.

"He wasn't always afflicted, you know." Miss Simpson pressed her lips together. "Afflicted," she thought, was the last word in the world to describe Daniel Colson when he first came to Kelseyville. "Graced," "Endowed," were more like it, —except for that selfish little wife. So able, so fine. No one in town understood—no one else. Miss Simpson took tucks and added gussets in her memories, and trimmed away unwanted material, discarding it like scraps. So sensitive—that year they served at the polls together—she always felt there was a bond of recognition though of course—.

"So what happened?" Beth urged.

"She simply deserted husband and child. He saw her to the stage coach, and had Ernie put her bags up for her. Lucy Burgess was Post Mistress then, and she told me Daniel never received so much as a post card from her."

The hatch was almost finished, and the tiny poults were already peeping and stirring about, their eyes bright with the pleasure of life. One poor baby had trouble: he had pecked a hole in the egg to get his head out, but had got tired out struggling with one leg that was doubled backward on him and dried stuck to the shell because of a tiny crack. Beulah wet that part with a rag dipped in the water pan, and picked the shell off for him. The leg dragged on the ground behind him, but soon he was busy like the others, picking at the damp mash and crumbled egg yolk and tipping his head back to drink down the sour milk. It was a perfect day for them, Beulah thought, not too sultry.

The leaves of the scrub oak the nest was under began to shake stiffly in the breeze, making a shifting dapple of sunshine like they had made in the mirror around her in her new dress. She started to get that whirling feeling, like she was on the verge but couldn't remember something. It was like she was heading right into a breeze that was sparkling the pear trees, and blowing petals around her in every direction. It started to make her dizzy, but then she had to stoop down to get two chicks out of the milk pan, which was shallow and no danger, but she sponged them off so they wouldn't smell sour, and after that she was all right again.

She started back to the house. Half way up there was a stretch of mesh fence that had been part of a chicken pen at one time. It was only about fifteen feet long, but a turkey hen had got stuck behind it, and was running frantically back and forth. As soon as it got to the support pole at one end, it would turn and run back to the other. Beulah tried to shoo it around the end, waving the spread out flaps of her kimono but it wouldn't go, and kept on running back and forth. She picked up a switch and lunged at it swinging, yelling "Go around it, you dumb bird!" The turkey ducked its tail down and raced hysterically beyond the end of the mesh. Beulah kept chasing it till it outran her.

She let herself back in the bedroom, panting slightly, but beaming. The women broke off talking. Miss Simpson finished one last seam, snipped the thread, and put the dress back on Beulah. Beth touched her hair up and did her makeup, but Beulah gazed at her garnished face in the mirror and asked Beth to take off the eye stuff because she didn't recognize herself with it. They all followed her out to the car, and Miss Simpson arranged her skirt so it wouldn't get crushed on the ride to the church with Pa and Ernie.

Beulah and Pa stayed in the ante room, outside the big double doors to the auditorium where guests were already seated. Mable, the organist, had stationed her daughter Irma at the door to tell them when to start down the aisle. A quartet from the choir sang "My Heart at thy Sweet Voice," and "Oh, Promise me," which set Beulah puzzling about what it meant when they said "and love unspeakable that is to be," just as Irma said, "Now!" Pa, who was waiting with his back propped against the wall to ease it, pushed off and got beside her, straight as he could and they were all set to start off with the first chords of the march.

It wasn't "Here Comes the Bride, short fat and wide," as Beulah had expected. This piece started with one bunch of notes repeating over and over, and going up a notch higher for every repeat. At the top it started the march part, only not heavy like "Here Comes." This tune rolled down bouncy, like a ball on a stairway. It made her feel like skipping, except for Pa.

Jess was way at the other end of the aisle, standing with the minister under an arched trellis covered with branches of quince and pear blossoms which Beulah thought was the prettiest thing. Jess's hair was slicked down to his head, and she could see he had a fresh haircut by the rim of white around his sunburnt tan. Even that far away she could see his eyes were real wide open and steady, and he was standing extra still, the way he always stood when he watched her come up the path to the stile, as though it was a wonder to see her there. He had on his brown suit which had got tight on him now he was a filled out man, and a new white shirt. She had offered to wash and iron up one he already had, but he said that wasn't right till they were married.

Mr. McGiven, the Methodist minister who was waiting under the arbor with Jess, looked pleased and cheerful, not scary the way Mr. Harper was when he talked about her and Jess getting married.

Pa liked Mr. McGiven even though he was a preacher, and she did too. He was big, with high, square shoulders. His nose took an almost square down bend where it had been broken in a fight, and his eyes looked sharp as steel, but still kind. Whenever there was a social, he made sheets of tiny buttermilk biscuits he had learned how to make when he was a cook in a lumber camp once. Beulah looked forward to those today, and all the rest. Pa had arranged for Mrs. Tallman to take charge of refreshments, so she knew they'd be good. She was getting hungry.

Almost everybody she knew was there, turned around backward to watch her and Pa coming down the aisle, and looking like they were glad to see them. It was easy for Beulah to walk slowly like they told her to, because she was used to walking with Pa, and besides it gave her a surer hold on her new Cuban heeled white shoes. These made her feel elegant and stately, and Mrs. Tallman, who was a big woman herself, whispered to Mr. Tallman she'd never noticed it before, but Beulah had a fine carriage. Between steps Beulah tried to tell how the baby was taking it, but she didn't get any sign.

Beth watched, thinking that whether she knew what she was doing or not, Beulah looked better in that peachy voile than she ever had in her life. Beth was sitting beside Miss Simpson at the back. She turned to look at her when she felt Miss Simpson raising her arm, slow and creepy, so you could tell she was trying not to attract any attention. Tears were running down her face, and she was wiping them away with her fingers. Kate, seated on the other side of her, noticed it too. When Miss Simpson finally gave in and lifted her handkerchief to both eyes, Kate, on the other side of her, started to put out her hand to touch her but decided against it. Beth watched her smothering her sobs for a moment, then looked at Kate and shrugged broadly.

Daniel Colson was watching his footing. With every step he took, the corner of his vision filled with Beulah's pink dress swirling over her new shoes. He thought of her first steps and first words, so long in coming, how hard it had been for him to face her limitation, how Ellie could not. He bumped against the side of the trellised arch after he turned her over to Jess and started to back off. Petals shook down from it into a strip of sun coming through the big windows. He remembered Ellie, hurrying away from him and the children through a shower of blossoms, holding her hat on with a raised arm. "Daniel," she said, "You've got to let me go. I can't stand it."

Beulah raised her face to the sunlit falling petals. Mr. McGiven bowed his head to watch them settling on his Bible.

Chapter 16

You were awfully hard on Izzy, Charlie, considering she hasn't done anything."

"Yeah well, that's one thing you're a lot better off doing something about before it happens instead of after."

Charlie slammed the door behind himself and walked out to the barn, his steps grating into the hard earth. He didn't have to go yet, but he certainly wasn't going to hang around while Vivian judged his performance. He could do that himself. He'd been a bastard, and treated Izzy as if she was a really bad kid. It didn't even make sense. He wanted her to be popular and have a good time while she was young because it looked like it was downhill fast once you were through school and out in this world. But under this his anger boiled and spat like lava as the picture of Izzy's head laid between the hoodlum's shoulders came back to him. His fist, and his body tensed as if he were really going to knock the kid out of his bike seat. He looked at the fist as if it didn't belong to him. He didn't need Viv bawling him out to make him feel bad about it. She was getting pretty good at that lately, goddamnit, just when he needed a little support. He felt like he'd have to blast a hole in his troubles and get out.

What he did was kick the door of the truck. It swung idly open and he got in and headed back to town. He'd meant to have lunch at home, to save his money, but he'd rather go hungry than sit there with Vivian thinking how right she'd been and how wrong he was.

He drove through the mesa brush without seeing anything except the windshield. A big jolt on his right front tire jerked the steering wheel in his hand and sent the truck into a sickening little slide to the right. It had to be a jack rabbit. There was nothing else in this territory he wouldn't have seen, but it must have been a record specimen. As if he didn't feel like enough of a shit already. Maybe it was his conscience he had just slithered over.

He let the gang at the shed load the truck while he scarcely even watched them. One of them said he must have gotten a kink in his disposition as well as his back.

As usual, lately, he rehashed his life as he drove the grade. It was like patting every inch of wall in the dark to find out where you were, and ending up more lost than ever.

When he finally got into Hopland he was so preoccupied he watched a woman cross the road with an armload of groceries without recognizing that it was Gloria till she reached the Star roadster. He drew up beside it.

"Hi," he said. It sounded like a bitter remark.

"Well, hello, Charlie!" She made it sound like an event. "I just came over to do the books here before the season heats up in Kelsey town. Come by for a beer after you unload."

"I'll see. Maybe." he said.

Charlie knew the house. What he hadn't realized seeing it from a distance, was how trim and well-cared for everything was. Neat as Giorgio. It didn't even fit into Hopland, it was so spruce and prosperous looking. Gloria had done fine by herself with her fruit tramp, he thought. He was wiping the dust from his shoes when Gloria opened the door.

She just said, "Come in, Charlie. I'm outside in the back yard. It isn't any cooler, but it's bigger." He followed her down the hall. She was wearing a pair of white pajama trousers, soft and wide enough to flow around her high heeled sandals as she walked, and a lilac blouse with wide easy-going ruffles at the V neck and wrists. She looked good—not so crisp as the way she dressed for work.

There were tall cottonwood trees in the yard. A pergola hung with wisteria was like a long shady room across the back of the house, cutting off the sight of the houses on the sides. White picket fencing edged the sides of the lawn as neatly as crochet, but there was no fence at the back where tall wild grass gradually gave way to brush and trees as the land climbed toward the western hills. Gloria poured him a beer. He took a sip, and raised his head with an appreciative grunt. There was no label on the brown bottle, but this was great beer. He wasn't even going to ask where she got it, because it was a cinch he couldn't afford it, even if he knew. He took another deep swig that left a moustache of foam on his upper lip which he left there for a minute feeling the bubbles pop while he watched the tiny chains of more bubbles pouring upward in his glass on the table. He got up to walk out onto the lawn and glance into the neighboring yards. Just back stoops and clotheslines on spindly poles. He stood gazing up into one of Gloria's cottonwoods.

"Did you ever eat one of these?" Gloria asked. As he started to turn toward her, she tossed a dark fruit at him, hard. He tilted his hand slightly to catch it. Come now, Gloria, he thought, I wasn't shortstop for being clumsy.

"No," he answered, examining the horny rind closely. He shot the thing back to her without looking up, "Have you?"

She muffed the catch, knocking it straight up into the air. They both lunged at it, laughing. Charlie caught it over her head. It felt hard, but he could tell it would be soft inside. He caught the scent of her perfume as they jostled, of flowers he didn't recognize, with something else, not so simple, all mingled with sun and warm skin and sweat. That was mostly his contribution, he supposed.

"You dope," Gloria scolded, "they're fragile." She took it from him carefully, halved it and cut pale green slices from the shell.

Charlie tasted one. The pulp was slimy smooth, delicious once you got used to that. There were long dark threads running through it, attached to hard dark nodules, tasting like pine wood. He wasn't sure what he thought about it.

"Some friends brought it to Mom from L.A. They called it an alligator pear."

Charlie took another slice, looking thoughtful and discriminating before he swallowed it. "More like tree-frog pear wouldn't you say?"

He had some more beer; it wasn't quite so cold, but it tasted better than ever. They both had a lot more beer. It was pretty nice to sit in the shade and laugh about some of the stunts they pulled in school; Gloria remembered a lot he had forgotten. They had some more beer, and Gloria talked about places she'd been, and what it was like in Honolulu.

"I'm glad to see all that travel didn't broaden you too much."

"Don't knock travelling, Charlie. It's great. Besides it makes Lake County look good again"

"That right?" he asked. "Sounds like I ought to try it."

He let his gaze travel out the back and up the hills. "What happened to your back fence, Gloria?"

"I don't know, I just didn't want it there, somehow. This way it keeps the neighbors out and lets the jack rabbits in, I guess."

He felt again the jolt and slither of the jack rabbit, under his wheel and reached for the beer, which had been replenished. "Well, I've got to see how Lake County looks right now," he said, finishing off his glass as he got up.

"How many times have you been over those hills, Charlie?"

"Oh, I travel a lot too. I just don't get anywhere," he said.

He rose neatly from his chair. "Thanks for the beer." Again he followed Gloria through the house, this time he bumped against the wall twice. At the front door, she turned to face him so abruptly he nearly ran into her. She propped her arms on his shoulders, clasping her hands behind his neck.

"When are you going to take me out, Charlie?"

Just as he used to, he looked down at her and said judicially, "Next year? I think."

Gloria smiled broadly. "That's what you think."

He drove off, actually with something of a flourish. It was fun, kidding around with Gloria again.

The truck seemed to take the curves gracefully; driving was a pleasure. He wheeled grandly around one of the horseshoe bends, and began a rhythmic swing through the reverse curve, only suddenly the truck was stuck going straight across both lanes, like a road block, and then it stalled. He started it and roared into reverse, to get back into his lane, and then jammed into low to get going again before anybody caught him in the queer maneuver. Nothing appeared on the road in either direction for a long time, not even a rabbit. Charlie crept along wondering exactly how many beers he'd had; he hadn't noticed. He was late, too. He'd stayed longer than he realized. He'd forgotten what a wallop good beer had. It sure had made him sleepy. When he got to a turn-off on the shady side of the hill, he pulled out on it for a snooze.

Chapter 17

It was long past dinner time when Charlie got home. Viv set out a plateful of food she'd kept warm in the oven.

"Thanks," he said. "Where's Isobel?"

"She went in to choir practice with Jeannie."

Charlie ate slowly, staring ahead thoughtfully, while Vivian worked. Stevie was asleep. The house seemed closed up, crabbed. He carried his plate to the sink. "My back's bad, I'm going to bed." Viv nodded with her head down and her arms stuck in the dish pan as though they were planted in cement.

He lay in bed turning on one side for a while, and then the other, trying to find an easy position, dropping into a murky, half sleep, looking through half-lidded, glazed eyes, and then jerking awake, getting more and more tired. The tension in his muscles relented a little, but it didn't change the way he felt. He went over his visit in Gloria's back yard again, but there was nothing left now of the fun; he couldn't figure out what he was doing there. Finally, like slipping into warm water, his body eased into sleep. He was with Gloria in a convertible driving toward the lake in their bathing suits. A head-high stand of corn showed up beside the road on the right, and suddenly they were in a boat, sailing along on top of the corn, exhilarated and hilarious. Then it wasn't sunny any more, and there was only porous brown rock jutting up against an overcast sky as far as he could see. The creek that ran beside the road had disappeared, and instead he saw foam-frilled runnels draining through the rocks everywhere, like the last of a big wave running back to the sea. That's where he was headed, to the sea, but he didn't seem to be getting any closer. The stuff he was walking on was brittle and jagged, and kept breaking away beneath him, but he had to hurry anyway. He could smell the sea now. It was cold, but he had to get to the water.

"Hey, where's the ocean gone!" he called, pretending it was a joke.

There wasn't anyone to answer him. He felt choked by loneliness like a thirst. He had to get to the water, even if it was salt.

Gloria was just stepping out of her bathing suit. Her body was strong, not willowy and slight like she looked in the fancy pajamas suit. He liked the firm feel of it as he pulled her toward him, and the struggling of her body against his. What she was doing was pulling his suit down so they stood naked together, and then they were down on warm sand. He was trying to get in but she was struggling again, to get her mouth down to him instead, and with its soft engulfing he gave over to her, the sound like lapping water pulling him to the brink. He got away in time and said "Let me in," like an order, and sank himself in her.

As the current sped he could hardly keep track of where he was. He pushed Gloria's hair away from her face to find her mouth, but it wasn't Gloria's thick hair, it was light gold hair, clinging to pale, delicate skin, Izzy's childish skin, almost blue white and thin. Her eyes were closed, and her small mouth shut, so peaceful you'd think nothing would wake her. As he hauled himself away, the deep pang ripped through him. Stumbling with terror, he started to run.

He woke face down with the wadded up pillow bunching one cheek. It took him a second to realize it had only been a dream, then he turned over on his back and started to let out sighs of relief so heavy they were almost groans. Pity and tenderness swept over him at the thought of Isobel's sleeping face, and sick disgust with his own grimace of pleasure. He reached out to get his shirt beside the bed to wipe his belly off, his face elongated with dismay as he scrubbed at his front and at the sheet.

Hell, it was just a dream, they couldn't hang you for that. He stuffed the shirt under the mattress and drifted back into remembrance of the pleasure he couldn't help.

Christian Endeavor let out early because the pastor had to leave. He apologized, using his deepest voice, "I have a call to make," and asked one of the older boys to lock up. The members straggled out wondering what to do till they were picked up by their elders. One boy emerged mimicking "I have a call to make," but mostly they left quietly, as though everything was over, Jeanne thought, like after a movie, though dusk still hung in the new dark. The only stars were two big round ones in the west, and it was warm, still. It felt to her like something was right on the verge of happening, instead of already over. Isobel came out the door after Jeanne, and the minute she did she saw Kenny leaning on the cottonwood by the road, watching as they came out. He started toward them, and she had a hard time holding back with the others, but she did, just looking at him till he reached them.

"You're out early," he said, matching the slow pace. "How come?"

"How come you even knew when we were supposed to be out?" Izzy asked.

"Research," he said, "but not believing it was what was smart. Why don't we go to Tallman's. I've got the car."

"Not me. I've got to wait for Irv," Jeanne said. "Anyway, that's him," she said as a car wheeled in the road and headed toward them. "I guess he's pretty smart too."

Irv's headlights caught the tall boy waiting with his charges. Outsider, he figured—leather shoes, instead of Keds or boots like the locals, and he stood with a loose ease that was different.

Jeanne went to the car. "Hi, Irv. Nice timing. Kenny wants to take Isobel for a soda."

"You too; everybody," Kenny put in.

"I've got orders," Jeanne sighed, getting in beside Irv. "Yeah, I guess we better get on."

Isobel, standing by, wide eyed, and with a sober expression, rippled the fingers along her scarcely raised hand when Jeanne turned and waved.

"Gee, I don't know if that's all right or not, Umps. What do you think?" Irv asked starting off slowly.

"I don't know either," Jeanne said. "It never came up before. Izzy never does anything she isn't supposed to do." She drew the last out thoughtfully. Looking back she could see Kenny stoop down to catch something Izzy was saying and laugh before he closed the door on her side of his roadster. "She might, though." The Nash still crawled along while Irv wondered what else he could do, till he reached the creek, where he gunned it enough to make a wake.

"Is this yours too?" Izzy asked when Ken got in behind the wheel.

"Mm hmm, well, my mother's, anyway. The bike isn't mine; everybody in the house here uses it. The owner has another one he's real particular about, but he sort of threw the Indian to the lions."

Isobel thought the roadster was wonderful; idling along in it with the top down it was like strolling together. She leaned her head back to watch the stars coming through the gauzy dark, one here, and then one there, though you couldn't tell when it happened, exactly. The one thing she thought was wrong with the car was that she couldn't ride with her arms around Ken's waist and her head on his back, the way she had to on the bike. She turned her head toward him and smiled when she thought of that, and he reached out an arm and pulled her closer. Tallman's was having a flurry of business, so Kenny and she got a tiny table near the door that looked like it was standing tip toe on its twisted wire legs. It brought their heads close to touching over their menus. Kenny read off the fancy sundaes and sodas for Isobel to choose.

She usually had root beer, or a float for celebrations since every one of the sundaes cost more than her week's allowance. It seemed dangerous even to consider the others, but tonight she chose maplenut, with fudge, and Ken ordered the same with extra nuts. Mr. Tallman wrote it down peacefully in the rolled up order book that looked small as a postage stamp in the midst of his fat and muscular bulk. His son Johnny was a great football star, and Mr. Tallman got a lot of satisfaction out of that.

"More nuts for you, too?" Isobel nodded.

A girl Isobel didn't know stopped at their table. "Hi, Ken," she said, waiting for him to look up, as though she was presenting a surprise. Casually, she carried a black leather motorcycle jacket over one shoulder that looked as dangerous to Isobel as if it was a slung rifle. The youth beside her waited with an indulgent smile.

Ken looked up, "Oh, hi Sylvie," he said, turning in his chair to face her. "You actually found Lake County."

The excitement and cheer drained out of Izzy's face. The casual ease of the others made her feel like the outsider, the awkward, uninvited guest. Ken turned back to her, "Honey, this is Sylvie. She was packing grapes in Tulare when we were there a couple of weeks ago. And this is Isobel, my girl, I hope, who lives here." Isobel felt her life return.

"And this is Brad, who lives in Lakeport, where he has serious undertakings," Sylvia said.

"Bum joke," Brad said, still with his elaborately tolerant air. He was tall, with curly fine hair very dark against his forehead's white skin, and thick lashes over clear gray eyes. Izzy had seen him at every funeral she had ever been to, which was three, helping his father who owned the undertaking parlor in Lakeport, moving flowers around, showing people where to park, and guiding late comers to the grave sides. He had seemed soft and childish, but now he was so handsome she said "How do you do," hastily because she was sure he would never have noticed her.

"Hello, Isobel." he said, and it sounded so easy, that the notion of any complication disappeared. All three of them were like that, Izzy thought, as if they knew something that made everything easy. She wondered if it had to do with knowing about making love, somehow. It was sure different from Lake County kids.

"Why don't you come for a ride with us when you finish. We're parked out in front."

"He's got his daddy's car." Sylvie said, grinning. "You'll like it."

"Do you want to?" Kenny asked, when they were gone.

"If you do," she answered, her voice was as nonchalant as she could make it.

Brad and Sylvie were waiting for them outside, in a long black hearse. Kenny stepped back to admire its gleaming length, centered himself in front of it to see the chrome, turned half gold by the street light lavished on the perfect circles of its lamps, tracing the radiator and swathing the figure on the hood ornament, and then looked in over Brad's shoulder, to admire the dash board of polished wood, and the burnished brass trimming the round faced instruments.

"Wow," he said finally. "I didn't know what I was missing."

He and Isobel got in to sit on a deep-padded bench at one side of the back compartment, lined in plush, of a brownish gray with a purplish cast, that was so luxurious you forgot how suitably gloomy it was, and the big Packard backed silently out onto the road.

Isobel was trembling, holding on to the edge of the bench. Kenny tightened his arm around her shoulders, "You all right?" he asked. She was, then. She didn't know what she thought about getting into a hearse until you had to, but Brad was the funeral parlor's official driver now, so she didn't see how there could be anything wrong about it. It was dreamy smooth, and so silent, just a low purr instead of the rattle bang sputter and stall sounds you got used to; it was almost like when your ears didn't work after a swim because they were full of water. When they reached the orchards outside town, the rows blurred, they went by so fast. It felt unreal, here they were just floating along inside, while outside the land was streaking by. She watched it go, fascinated. She'd never seen it go by like that.

At the wheel, Brad didn't look like he was speeding. He looked relaxed and sociable as he took a flask shaped bottle out of his pocket, and raised it. "Anybody?" he asked, waiting a little for an answer, giving it a little shake when nobody spoke up. Then he took a long pull out of it himself and handed it to Sylvie, who held it before her on her knees, watching the road intently.

Brad lowered his window and leaned his head part way out. "Hey, Kenny," he hollered above the wind that lashed in, "You drive, will you, I want to try something." He stopped the big machine smoothly, and came around and opened Sylvie's door. "Do you mind riding in back, for a little? There's something I've been wondering about."

Kenny got in the driver's seat, wobbled the shift gear, and located the emergency brake. He glanced back at Izzy, who was making room for Sylvie on the bench before he started off. Brad leaned out his window, watching the moonlit landscape drifting by, his right arm hung over the side to his armpit. As they approached an oak growing near the road, he shagged a stone from his pocket at its trunk. It sailed silently into the field beyond. "Take it a little slower, Ken, would you please?" They passed hay fields, bleached pale by the moon, with an occasional oak towering black against them.

More of Brad's stones vanished silently. Brad reached into the puckered leather side pocket on the door and brought out a gun with a small barrel, longer than an ordinary pistol. A triangular road sign came into view. He aimed and followed it with great deliberation a moment before he fired. Zuiiiiing, the sound of a successful hit wound of into the night.

"That's interesting," he said. They were back among orchards again. Ziiiing, the next target, a hanging sign, saying The Oaks, and trimmed with pictures of acorns, responded. Brad said, "Let's get the Burma Shave ad on the Finley Road. You know where it is, don't you Ken?" He went on scanning the moon-bright roadside for fair game.

Charlie woke up with a start as though something had frightened him. After a few minutes lying on his back with his hands clasped under his head, staring at the ceiling with wide open eyes, with a stubborn set to his mouth, he stirred uneasily. Viv was still up. He could see the rim of light from the kitchen under the bedroom door. On his way to the bathroom he could see her sitting at the table, stitching the hem of a skirt.

"What are you doing up?" He heard a slur in his voice, and it's cold tone, like the voice parents use to a child in Dutch with them.

"Waiting for Isobel to get home." Vivian didn't look up to answer him.

"Till after eleven! What the Christ were you waiting for." He rammed back into the bedroom and pulled on his clothes.

"Now what are you going to do Charlie?"

"I'm going to look for her, naturally."

"Irv drove the kids in because Bill was away," he said. "He might be having trouble with the Nash, not being used to it."

"Yes, and Isobel might be having trouble remembering she's supposed to be in at a decent hour, too, the way she is lately."

"Oh, Charlie, she isn't 'any way' lately. It's you who are. But she probably needs a ride home all right."

He slammed the kitchen door, and Viv could hear the clang to the truck door, when he slammed that too.

Izzy leaned forward close to Kenny's back, as though she was huddling with cold. "I'm scared, Kenny," she whispered miserably. He gave a short downward nod, and drove on at an even rate, and though Izzy had thought they must be miles from town, shortly they turned into Main Street and pulled up before Tallman's.

Brad protested it was not time to quit, he was just really beginning to get the hang of it.

"We've got to get home now," Ken said evenly.

"Knock-out machine, Brad. See you, Sylvie." He handed Izzy out her side, and kept his arm close around her waist as they walked. Her hair haloed gold around her face in the light from Tallman's windows. She thought she had never in her life seen anything so cool and masterful as the way Ken had gotten them away without making any fuss.

"I'm sorry he scared you, Honey. He's just a goof-ball, but that machine is a dreamboat. I'll bet his Dad's customers never had it so good, if they just knew it."

Worried as she was, Izzy had to giggle when he said that. They got into Ken's model A parked at the corner.

It looked suddenly very small and plain, and when they started up, the rattle and bumps she hadn't even noticed before seemed so awful she laughed again. Ken pretended to sulk at the insult to his car, and drove toward the creek so slowly the rattles were unrecognizable, and eased into the water without a splash. With the roadster's top down, they could feel the cool moist stir in the air. Ken slowed almost to a stop to mingle with the moon-path. Izzy felt drenched in dazzle through and through. He pulled her closer to his side, so they swayed as one while the little car waddled over the stony bed. Izzy wished it would last forever, but soon the car was crawling out of the water and up the opposite rise.

At the top, a truck was bearing toward them, seeming to fill the whole road as they leveled out. Isobel recognized it with a sickening return to earth.

Charlie stopped and got out. He seemed headed toward Ken's side of the Ford, but Izzy cried "Papa!" and he veered to her side.

"Where the hell have you been?" His voice had the sound of grief and betrayal in it, as well as fury.

"Oh, Papa," Isobel pleaded, "we only went for a little ride with Brad Jones, but he kept going on and on. Ken got us away as soon as he could."

Charlie opened her door and grabbed her by the elbow, steering her stumbling over the ruts back to the truck.

"Get in," he said, boosting her high by the arm so she was shoved against the door frame, scraping her shoulder as he crammed her into the truck. Her head struck the cab's roof jolting back on her neck.

"Don't you dare hurt her," Kenny yelled, scrambling out of the roadster, stumbling as he ran to help her.

Charlie slammed the truck door and started back for Ken at a plodding pace, saying "What did you say?" in the same measured way, as though he couldn't believe what he heard. It seemed more threatening than if he had raged. Izzy jumped down from the truck and ran to cut him off. "Papa don't" she screamed.

"I said don't hurt her," still yelling, Kenny came on. He looked like a figure made of twigs compared to Charlie. Isobel threw her arms around both of Charlie's, falling against him, and was dragged to her knees. Charlie stopped still, as if her arms really pinned him. "Papa, are you crazy!" Izzy sobbed.

He looked down at her head. "Get up," he said in a dull voice, and headed back to his truck. Izzy hurried to get in. As she opened the door, she could see Ken still standing in the road. He looked as though he wanted to cry.

"Well, here she is," was all Charlie said to Viv when they got home. He went off into the bedroom with the funny upright stride he had when he was trying to hide the back pain. He could hear Izzy sobbing as she talked, and then quieting, and after awhile Viv came to bed, making controlled, quiet movements not to wake him, while he lay so rigid faking sleep he felt petrified, even keeping from blinking till his eyeballs dried, staring at the same brownish cone of darkness in front of his face. Finally Viv cautiously turned onto her side away from him, and he heard her breathing fall into the regular rhythm, like slow waves toppling, of real sleep. When finally he fell asleep his body made a big floppy jerk and then lay sprawled as though it had fallen from a height.

What woke him was Vivian's voice in the next room, crying, "Charlie! Charlie! Izzy's gone," she said in a choked-off voice when she saw he was awake.

He heaved himself up on one elbow, squinting in the thin dawn light. "What?" His face went yellow as tobacco stain.

"Packed and gone. With Kenny, I guess."

Charlie collapsed back down on the bed. "Christ, Vivian, for a minute I thought you meant she was dead."

Viv stood looking down at him. "Isn't this bad enough for you?"

"Yeah, it is," he said, but he felt luxurious with relief. He got up and dressed in the clothes he'd left on the chair and floor, trying to think what he was going to do.

"I never heard a thing. He must have come back for her after we were asleep." Viv kept going over the circumstances. Irv had been the one who went in to pick the girls up; Bill would have known not to leave without Isobel.

"That stuff doesn't matter," Charlie said. He was busy, checking his denim jacket for car keys, and wallet, shifting his tobacco sack to his shirt. He poured himself a cup of coffee in the kitchen, and drained it, then turned and went out the door, as though where he was going was nobody's business but his own.

The door banged twice behind him, and Viv grabbed his arm. "What are you going to do?"

"Find her, I hope."

"How?"

"How do I know." He pulled his arm away, got into the Ford and set the spark and choke slowly. Then he had to look at her. He couldn't just storm off as though she was to blame, but he could hardly get his head to turn to face her. Her wrapper was pulled tight across her shoulders and chest. It made them look frail, and her waist seem solid and unyielding. Her hair was pinned up on top of her head, with curly strands loose around her face, her eyes burning blue with distress, beseeching him, as though he could fix everything if he only would.

"Don't scare her away, Charlie," she said. He wanted to hit her, and bent his head in disgrace with himself, watching his foot stomp harder and harder on the starter, till the engine caught and he could get away.

Very calm and businesslike he knocked at the door of the house on Main Street where Kenny lived. Several men, all a few years older than Ken, were getting ready for work. One took off on the motorcycle Charlie had assumed was Ken's. At least Isobel wasn't out on the road on that thing.

Ken's car was gone, they said. No one had any idea when he had left. Nobody knew whether he owned the car or not.

Charlie said "Thanks," and drove away briskly. He rode southeast a long time through the familiar blur of pines and underbrush and drying grass, till the road divided, and he had to decide whether to head toward Lower Lake or over the mountain to Calistoga. He pulled off the road and sat. Beside him, upright on the trunk of an old oak, on a wounded spot the bark had shrunk away from, a woodpecker was busy pounding still another acorn into bare gray wood already thickly studded with them. He turned a round yellow eye on Charlie, briefly, and then returned to his task, his head pounding like a jack hammer. Charlie sat watching. Fool Bird, he thought, you don't know what you're doing any more than I do. After a while, he started the car up again, turned around in the road, and headed back to Kelseyville.

Chapter 18

Beth ducked her head to catch all her hair under the white towel then twisted the ends into an elegant high turban. She thought her skin looked great against the absolute white. If you stayed out of the sun all you could in Lake County, you got just the right kind of tan anyway. She was lazy after the swim and shampoo. Here she was with a real date with Bill coming up, and she didn't want to move a muscle to get ready, because it was so just good to sit still and realize that finally he had asked her for one, to dinner in Lakeport before the movies, and even asked her ahead of time, instead of almost the last minute, as though it was accidental.

She turned her head three-quarters to the mirror, and to the side and looked out into the garden. What ever caused it, it was wonderful to have Bill treating her like she was his girl. She would wear her pale yellow Indian Head. It had that easy, cool look, almost like it was linen, and wouldn't look too dressed up. She didn't want Bill to imagine she thought anything special about the night. She'd wear her white clip at the neck—the little flowers it was made of were enamel, so it was sporty, but there was a tiny rhinestone in the center of each one, so it was extra pretty. It would go with her white sandals, too. She imagined the way Bill would be talking, wound-up explaining something to her, he wouldn't even notice how she was dressed. That was Bill, but he would trail off, talking, looking at her.

"My God, you're pretty," she could hear him saying it suddenly, like it was surprised out of him.

She would shake her head slightly, abstracted as if she didn't want to lose the thread of what he was telling her. When they finished dinner he would get out a cigarette, looking at her while he bounced it hard on the table cloth like he did to shake down the tobacco. His eyebrows would be raised in round arches, and his eyes sparkling with that "What's next, world?" look he had, then he would put the cigarette down unlit beside his plate, and reach right across the table to take her hand, and say, "Let me just look at you." She'd waited a long time for Bill to look at her like that.

She'd sit close to him driving home, without talking, because after holding hands all through the movie, they'd be just about overcome by the fire running between them. Bill would take her home, but when he started to kiss her good night, she could tell he wasn't going to stop, but she would draw away, after a couple of minutes, though letting him see she was all worked up too, and say she had to go in. She wouldn't want Bill to think she was easy.

She got up and pulled the cretonne curtain of her closet aside and shot the wire hangers zinging along her closet pole, leafing through the clothes to be sure the yellow dress was really what she wanted to wear. She pulled it out when she came to it. As she turned to toss it on the bed, she caught a glimpse of herself in the bureau mirror in her step-ins.

Something looked different, good. She turned sideways again to catch it. Her breasts had a tipped-up look, as though the crinkled dark nipples were partly holding them up in a way she'd never noticed before, and they looked bigger. Facing the mirror she tested her hips and waist with a couple of pinches to see if she was getting fat. She wasn't, at least not there. Then it came over her what Ma had said about breasts first showing any change.

She felt everything come to a stop, as though the blood in her veins suddenly froze. She stared at the mirror, dates and figures tumbling in her head, but she couldn't remember any for sure. Watching the mirror, she turned sideways again, to check if she was seeing things, but it was still all there. Everything got dark around that spot of mirror, and she put out an arm to brace herself. She hadn't ever fainted, but maybe she might. Nothing would surprise her now. She could just imagine herself with a squalling baby on her hip, milk stains darkening her dress around one nipple, the way she had seen a fruit tramp, once, who had to work overtime and couldn't get to her kid till his dinner was overdue. She needn't worry about that, though; Pa would kill her long before that. She put on a tight smile, but her face paled. That vein on Pa's neck would probably blow then and there, if he ever found out.

Her heart was pounding like a flat tire. She better calm down or Ma would notice it the minute she saw her, and anyway, she didn't have time to get flustered and make any wrong moves. Her dream of marrying Bill started to look pretty dim in the face of this thing, though Bill was the kind that would go straight through to marrying you if he did knock you up, that was Bill, but it was fat chance that anybody could trick Bill. What necking he did was always just good night at the door or somewhere else he could make a quick get-away if he needed to. Bill would make a perfect father. Nobody in town would have a word to say, then. They all thought a baby was great stuff, so long as you had a ring to go with it. She halfway laughed and choked on a sob. When you were in this condition you couldn't be choosy about what you did, she was beginning to see that.

Probably the smartest thing would be to get rid of it, right away, but she didn't know what to do, or know anybody that did, for that matter. Muriel or her mother probably would, since they were both whores. Muriel always stayed separate from the others in school. She would go eat her lunch under a tree, near the crowd that settled on the steps, or the tennis courts, but she never tried to join. Still you could tell she was sort of a good soul: she could ask Muriel. And then she saw by the look on her face in the mirror that she would-n't. All the whispered stuff she'd heard about abortions seemed to be trying to get into her head at once, and she couldn't face the thought of it. She'd rather die in childbirth than that way.

She sat down on the bench at her dressing table, remembering Earl. The double-dyed bastard, his wallet had a circle worn on it where he carried condoms, but because she was fighting him off that night it had been too much bother for him. She didn't have time to waste getting sore at Earl again. She had to think what to do.

She went back to the closet and leafed through her clothes again, slowly, and finally picked out the one outfit Bill had ever said he liked. She'd have to at least try for Bill. She was crying.

She ran down the path to get in the Nash quick when Bill stopped in front. She certainly didn't want Pa to get into the picture on this date. Bill leaned over and shoved the door open, smiling so his teeth showed white against his tanned skin. His hair looked extra dark and curly, because it was still sopping wet, as if he hadn't even toweled it after his shower. His eyes sparkled their double colors. Pa would say he looked like a wop, if he could see him. He said that when he wanted to discount somebody even though he had married one hisself. With all the summer-dark tan and the wet, he did look like an Italian, and a happy one.

She couldn't help answering his big smile, no matter how shaky she was feeling. "You look like you just found a million dollars," she said.

"All I found was a job. It just felt like a million."

"A job where?' Her question was quick and urgent like she was jumping at him, and her voice was tense and small. She hated the sound of it.

"The City, well, part of the time in Imperial Valley and Brentwood where their other ranches are, but mainly in the sales office in Frisco."

"I thought you liked farming."

"Yeah, I do, but I'd also like to earn a living."

"But, aside from the money, what would it have to do with farming?"

"I'd be handling shipment and sale of all those crops, where all the work pays off. That's what's great about the produce game. Doing that right makes the difference between making a killing or losing your shirt. They already gave me a Railroad Guide, all the freight time tables and connections in America to 'look over,' which is polite for 'learn it.' And what do you mean, 'aside from the money'? There's no such place as 'aside from the money.'"

He talked on excitedly about how agriculture was real business now, had to be, particularly in California; how refrigerated freight cars had opened up the whole country to fresh produce from California. The old home farms didn't stand a chance, and particularly not in isolated places like Lake County with only a few crop possibilities, and no real farming tradition. Beth felt herself receding to a tiny point in a lost distance, huddling over the wretched secret in her belly, and the idea that she could get Bill to marry her seemed just a ridiculous pipe dream.

Bill looked over at her. "I'm boring you."

She managed to get out a polite murmur, as she shook her head. She was glad he was so steamed up talking about the future that she didn't have to talk, because what she felt like saying was "You're not boring me, you're killing me."

By the time they got to Lakeport, her scheme for the evening seemed so far in the past that the fix she was in her didn't seem so real either. Bill said he'd like to eat at the hotel, so he could see Konocti once from a different perspective. They went in and sat down at a table with two places set out on the white cloth by a window. It was up on a hill, and the menu had a picture of the lake with Konocti at the back so sooty and blurred that you caught your breath when you looked out the window at the real thing, with the lake shining dark as pewter, and the trees and fields quiet in the evening light, and Konocti climbing straight out of it, its top still red with sun. She hadn't eaten dinner out in a hotel before, but she didn't have anything to be afraid of. Ma gave banquets in their own dining room for outside parties, and everybody that came to them said that was the best place in the county to eat. Ma always had the table set for their own dinners just the same as if it was for one of the parties so she knew how to act. Bill looked pleased as he ordered a coke to go with dinner. She knew exactly the sort of red wine that would go with the dinner that was laid out on the menu. It made her feel sort of elegant to know what would have been perfect with it, even though you couldn't get any wine at all at the hotel because of Prohibition. She sipped her coke, which the waitress brought right away like it was an emergency, and it did seem to pick up her spirits almost as if it was wine, so she raised her glass to Bill like a toast. As she drank to it, she realized that her face had on a merry, sweet look she could never in the world have put on if she tried. It just came naturally with the gesture because she had seen her mother look the same way a hundred times when she would give a toast, or get one for her good dinners.

In answer, Bill made a big flourish, and saluted her with his glass. Someone would think she had something to celebrate. She laughed when she thought that, and Bill was feeling so good he laughed too. Suddenly she was in the mood for a celebration, no matter what. Dinner was good, and they ordered desert with the feeling they could have anything in the store. Maybe it was partly because she felt like she didn't have anything to lose anymore, but whatever it was she felt easy with Bill. After the movie, Bill asked her if she would like a soda, or something, but then he remembered he had to pick up Umps after Christian Endeavor, and said they better get back to Kelseyville. They could all go to Tallman's, which would beat any place in Lakeport, anyway. He was going to miss Tallman's.

Bill walked her around to the back door when they got home, which at least was out of sight of Jeanne. The truck was gone, so she didn't have to worry about Pa storming out to yell at her, either. It came over her all at once that this might be the last time she ever saw Bill, even though he'd come home to see his folks sometimes, she supposed. She let her head drop so the tears in her eyes wouldn't make her mascara run, but Bill lifted her chin up with a finger, the way you would to make a child tell the truth, and kissed her long and softly, as though he was yearning and hating to separate just like she was. Then he held her to him a long time, as if it was cold outside the circle their arms made. He kissed her again, finally, a stamp-and-seal, finishing kind of kiss, and turned away quickly. She could barely make out that he said "I'm sorry," as he turned away to go because it was under his breath, as though he was saying it to himself.

She felt empty and idle, listening to the sounds of the Nash dwindling away. Her body slackened, and she leaned back against the door instead of going in, feeling her old dreams crumbling around her, everything narrowing down. If she cut Bill out of her thoughts, there wasn't much good left to think about. With Bill for a father, the baby would have learned how to be somebody. He would just naturally make something of himself from being around Bill, even though he was Earl's. She might have amounted to something herself, to keep Bill. Going with him was the best thing that ever happened to her, even though there hadn't been very much to it. The last sound vanished when the Nash went over the crest at the cross roads. She went in, then, careful not to let the door bang and wake Ma, but as she passed her mother's room she heard the heavy creaking of the bedspring like Ma was just getting onto it. She must have been praying, down on her big knees by the bed the way she did. If she only knew the trouble her daughter was in, she'd pray overtime for her, that was for sure. God knows her daughter could use any help she could get. She sure wasn't getting anywhere by herself.

Chapter 19

Viv made a special trip to town for the mail. She could see a letter when she looked through the glass in the door of the Norton box on the bottom deck of the small bronze crypts that lined one wall of the P.O. and brushed Steve's hand away from the box, and hastily dialed the combination herself, overshooting one of the numbers so she had to dial twice. She leaned her bent head against the wall of boxes as she ripped the envelope open.

Dear Mama and Papa,

Please don't be too mad at me and Ken. I was afraid Papa would hurt him and even me, though I knew he would be sorry after. I know he will think this is ten times as bad. We tried to get married but they said I was too young without your consent, so we will just pretend to be, until I am old enough. I just wanted you to know I am safe. Please don't hunt for us, it would only do harm. I promise I will write.

Your loving daughter,
Isobel

For a minute, Viv was relieved. They would find Izzy and bring her back home and everything would be all right again. She came down to earth soon. Things wouldn't be the same, even when they found her. She felt helpless in the pull of a long loss, some down curve they were all on that she couldn't fight. Besides, she hardly knew what 'the same' meant, anymore. There used to be one feeling that connected all of them no matter what, but now there was such a jumble of resentment, and disappointment she didn't know what she felt, except guilty to even think such a thing. She'd been so busy with Stevie, and with trying to make ends meet, she'd left Isobel to shift for herself, just because she was such a thoughtful kid. She ached with apology for doing that. And now she'd gone her own way.

One thing she knew was that Charlie wouldn't hurt the children, even though she hardly knew what else to expect from him one day to the next. He was glum so much of the time she'd got used to it. Everything he said was shaded and double edged. She couldn't tell whether he was being sarcastic or not anymore. She hadn't understood Izzy either, apparently. They'd gotten to be on guard with each other, somehow. She saw herself suddenly, kind of grim and curt, laying down the law for Izzy. When she thought about the family, she didn't recognize herself—except with Stevie.

Charlie must have really scared Izzy to death to make her react like that. Out of the blue Viv pictured Helena, straight and proud on her horse at the head of the parade, and remembered how Charlie turned away in disgust when he recognized her. "That's a hell of an example," he'd said, but she had taken that as a sort of joke, Charlie's style. She tried to remember his face when he said that, but she couldn't see it, not really. She didn't know what Charlie thought anymore. She had never seen him so worked up as he was over those rides Izzy took with Ken. Being moody was one thing, but scaring Izzy like that was going too far.

Anger colored her face as she pegged along the street to the car with Stevie trotting to keep up with her, and drove down into the creek crossing so fast the flivver stalled. She was sitting and wondering if the engine was hot enough to dry itself off, or if she would have to wade, when a truck rattling with a load of empty boxes dipped down to the crossing and pulled even with her.

Jimmy Gunn hopped out to wipe off the carburetor and check the magneto for her, looking as though a nicer thing couldn't have happened. That made her laugh, so that her anger eased up, but her vague guilt persisted.

Charlie was in the courtyard carrying his stuff out to the truck when she got home. She handed him the letter without saying anything, and Steve looked wonderingly from one to the other of them while Charlie read it silently.

"Oh, Jesus," he said. He heaved an enormous sigh through his nose. Viv watched him. "Oh, Jesus," usually meant he was exasperated and feeling sorry for himself. Was that all it came to, for Charlie? She felt deserted and helpless when Charlie didn't take hold, as though she was stuck holding up a wall by herself.

"What are we going to do?" she said in a flat, harsh voice. "We've got to find her before she gets in worse trouble."

"Yeah, sure," Charlie said, antagonism quick in his voice. "And how are you going to find her if she doesn't want to be found? The State Patrol might trace the car? If we knew who owned it, but God knows who that is. It's a cinch he doesn't."

"I don't want to have the police hunting them like they were criminals," Viv said hotly.

"Well, do you want to find them or not? If you like it better the way it is, we'll skip it."

"I don't like it at all. I think it's awful. I can't imagine what you did to scare her so bad."

Charlie glared at her. "That's it, huh. Whole thing boils down to what did I do wrong, as usual. Did it ever occur to you that you might do something wrong once in awhile?"

He strode over to his truck and got in. He stared down at his foot on the starter while it ground reluctantly a while before the engine caught. Viv ran up to the cab and hooked her hands over the door, supplicant.

"Oh, Charlie, don't just go off like that. I didn't mean anything. I was just trying to think."

Charlie twisted his head away from her to look through the small window in the rear of the cab, and gunned the truck backward in a big arc. He jounced out the driveway to the road without a glance in her direction. He'd felt like pulling the young pup out of his roadster and breaking his head in, but actually, he'd done absolutely nothing, as usual. Surely, Izzy knew he'd rather lie down in front of the truck at its customary slow speed than hurt a hair of her head. Yet she hadn't trusted that, and she'd done something about it. She'd run off with a tramp, and she planned to keep running, for what? two more years? That is if Ken didn't run out on her and leave her stranded pregnant somewhere.

That wasn't giving Ken much credit, considering he didn't know anything against the kid, beyond the fact that he was a fruit tramp. At least he was one of the fancy ones that rented rooms instead of camping out beside some creek.

They were both so young! A spear of tenderness pierced him. They seemed like babies, as he thought of them, and yet, there they were, standing up together in the license office, running together to a common life and bed—not just away from him.

Whatever he had done to separate them was trivial compared to what was pulling them together, anyway. What a way to lose Izzy, before she'd learned what anything was about or how to handle herself, as though she'd crawled down from his lap one day and eloped the next. The time between was a blur, a consistent downgrade. He couldn't even see Viv, she had disappeared in the monotony. Yet when he and Viv were the age of Izzy and Ken, nothing could have kept them apart. He knew that as a fact, as if somebody had told him, or he'd read it. He'd lost the real memory. The years circled tighter around him, binding him. The only new element was Gloria, his own little fruit tramp.

Well, that sure slipped in accidentally, he thought, but it was true. Gloria and Ken were the same breed. He would have done better probably to scare Gloria away, instead of Izzy, if he'd become such a living threat, except Gloria didn't scare easily. He saw Izzy's pale worried face and winced, then told himself scornfully, "Don't be silly. She's probably rolling in bed with her tramp right now." He started to remember his dream, and his thoughts closed like curtains, leaving him only the road, the truck, and the fact that he was running a little behind schedule.

Chapter 20

Stevie nudged his plate a few inches away from him, climbed off his chair, and started for the door with determined steps. His purposeful air, what Charlie called his "single track," amused Charlie. "Where you going, Son?" he asked.

"I'm going to throw up," Stevie said.

He didn't eat, and said his stomach hurt, but once he was in bed looking at his books, he said he was all right. Around dawn he came to the open door of his parent's room, "Mama," he called. Viv could see him outlined by the faint light, bent over and holding his middle with both arms. She pulled on the light over the headboard and hurried to him. Stevie, raised his damp, grayish-pale face and said, "Help."

He threw up the water with a little baking soda in it she gave him, and lay back exhausted in the crib which was barely long enough to hold him, now. Occasionally he slept, twitching and jerking awake again with his hair drenched dark and clinging to his forehead but by morning he fell into a gentle sleep, his face smoothed out, with a little color, and his forehead cool to touch.

Charlie was relieved, almost buoyant, as he climbed into his truck, ragging Viv for being a worry-wart and telling her to get some rest herself. Viv was relieved too, and her cup of coffee eased her further. When she went to make their bed, she let fatigue pull her back into it.

Both she and Steve slept till past noon. He didn't want any lunch, but she thought that was probably just as well. He stayed in his crib, dozing off and on. Once when she felt his forehead, she thought the fever was coming back, though he still looked pretty good. He felt even hotter, the next times she checked, and while she was watching him, he began to twist and moan in his sleep.

She put him into his bathrobe and carried the long tube of him pressed in her arms with his toes dangling to her shins, out to the Ford, and bedded him down on the back seat with pillows and blankets.

Doc Masters' office in his square concrete house on Main Street was still cool. The doctor had retired five years before, but since there was no other in town he grudgingly accepted emergency visits. There was a little dust on the sills and cabinets, though no more than a week's worth, and a big blue fly trapped in a square glass jar, labeled "Sterile," containing a few balls of graying cotton, climbed the side, to buzz and flail at the top and then drop back. A bleak wave of hopelessness washed over Vivian as she watched the old doctor's impassive face as he tested Steve, pressing his tender belly with his hands stacked one on the other, checking twice where Stevie winced.

"Well, I'd say there's nothing definite. Keep him in bed and on liquids for a little. See how it goes."

Steve seemed heavier in her arms on the way out, but she was so glad to get out of the hopeless office that for a moment she felt sure everything was going to be all right.

"Thank goodness that's over, huh Stevie" she said, as she tucked him into the improvised nest. The dry air carried the scents of sage and tar weed as they ran through the mesa, and of wet earth in the irrigated orchards, when they turned down to the Rincon again.

Steve was quiet, asleep, she thought, and she was sorry to have to wake him when they reached home. As she started to get out of the car, she glanced back at him. His jaws were clenched and he watched her tensely. Suddenly he jackknifed to a sitting position. "Mama" he screamed.

She got one arm under him and felt his face burning against her throat as she held him to her while she shoved the pillows and blankets to the car floor. While she nested him down in them, she heard her crooning voice telling him that they were going to go right over Cobb Mountain to the St. Helena hospital where they would take care of him, and that he must lie still as could be so as not to hurt himself, and keep the blanket over him so he wouldn't get chilled. When they got to the Hospital, he'd see the difference in what a real up and coming doctor was like. He'd see. Just a little while now, and he'd get some real help. Her voice wove a soft lining to the cocoon of blankets around Steve, while her terror and dismay nearly choked her. She wheeled the Ford around in the courtyard and headed back to town and the main road.

It was possible Charlie might be getting back from Hopland around now. If he stopped for the mail or to look in at the pool hall a minute, she might be able to catch him. They really needed the truck to get over the mountain; the flivver was too old to count on. She needed Charlie to do the driving so she could hold Stevie and take care of him.

She pushed into the clicking dusk of the pool hall. "Has anybody seen Charlie?" she asked at large. "Stevie's got to go to the hospital."

One of the regulars at the hall answered her. "It looked like his truck out in front of the Graham place when I went by a little while ago."

"Thanks." It was a half mile out of, her way, but they needed the truck.

As soon as she could see the house, she recognized Charlie's truck in front of it. Charlie probably had stopped to straighten out some load records with Mrs. Graham. That was the best luck all day. She ran up the cement steps to the porch. The screen door was hooked, and didn't give enough to rattle when she tried it. She pushed the paint-crusted doorbell and listened for its sound. What she heard instead, from the window with a drawn blind on her left, was Charlie's low chuckle, and a woman's voice, young and teasing, then muffled and cut off in mid-sentence, and the creak of bed springs shifting with a change of weight, then creaking regularly. The fist she had raised to knock on the door dropped to her side. Her pounding heart was as loud in her ears as the murmur of Charlie's voice mingling unintelligibly with the woman's. She stood bewildered, turning to go, then turning back again. The voices stopped, and only the bed sound pulsed on. She turned finally and went down the steps, her shoulders hunched over as if she was ashamed of herself. She tested Steve's forehead with her hand; he moved his head a little, as though to escape her touch so he could concentrate. His breathing was shallow.

"We won't be long, honey, we'll get there right away now fast as we can go." Her feet seemed too heavy to move, but she got them to the car door, and got in. She headed for the highway, thinking only about the route to take, weighing the time the mountain short cut might save against its risks, as though her mind had focused like a spotlight on the task, obliterating everything else in darkness.

At the Cobb Mountain turn off, she hesitated a second before she chose the sparsely gravelled road through the pine meadows at the mountain base, the old 'short' route. Within a few yards she hit a pot hole that jolted the Ford sickeningly and made Steve moan. "Oh honey, we won't hit any more mean holes like that, I promise you. We'll stay on the highway where its nice and smooth, and we can go fast." She had forgotten how rough the back roads were. She reversed into the grass beside the narrow road, and fled back to the highway. At the junction, a woodpecker launched itself from the side of a pine, and flew across her path. She gave a little gasping laugh. The flurry of wings seemed like a fist full of feathers shaken before her face to scare her.

The tight hold she held on her thoughts was loosened by the laugh. Maybe it hadn't been Charlie at all. Maybe he had loaned the truck to somebody. Irv, Bill's visitor, that was it, with some young girl. Then she admitted to herself how silly she was being. She knew Charlie when she heard him; she could recognize even his sneeze as far as she could hear it.

Driving the newly scraped highway, smooth and speedy under the Ford by comparison, her spirits lifted briefly, then chilled when the first shadows cut off the western sun and the fears she had kept distant closed in. Maybe it wasn't a good sign that Stevie was so quiet, maybe he was getting too weak to fight. She had gotten just far enough to be almost exactly midway between the two towns, and it was getting late.

Anybody on the road at this hour would be headed home. If she had trouble, she would be stranded in no-man's land. Gas. It was a cinch she would need more. She'd have to go into Lower Lake for it—another half-mile off course. Remembrance of her other half-mile detour jarred the careful cover she had kept on it, and all her grief blended into one black mound blurring her vision, smothering her breath. The lengthening shadows were becoming part of her, like an encroaching numbness.

A sound like the near miss of a bullet brought her alert in time to fight the veering steering wheel as her left rear tire blew out. Even as she struggled with the tool box and the spare tire mounted on the back she admitted to herself it was a waste of time. The tire had a slow leak they hadn't been able to locate; it was only good for a few miles. Still, it might increase her chance of getting help on the road if she could get even a little nearer to Lower Lake. She busied her hands, tearing at the tire in frustration, conscious of Steve's sick little body, worsening while she failed.

She should have got a shotgun and made old Doc Master take Stevie to St. Helena in his fancy brown and tan Marmon.

She should have kicked down the door and hauled Charlie off Gloria, that's who it was, of course! Gloria using her mother's house like that while the old lady was at the shed working, and got the keys to the truck, even if she had to drive it herself.

Another battered flivver, heading in the direction of Kelseyville, stopped opposite hers. The old man at its wheel, kept shaking his head sadly as she told him about Steve.

"Ain't a thing I can do," he said. "My old heap's as useless as yours, but I'll get you some help."

Sooner than she had dared hope, his old car showed up again, with a truck following him. The old man anxious to tell her how he had remembered he had heard a buzz saw whining when he passed the meadow headed the other way, and had caught the truck just as the logger was starting home.

Scott jumped out of his truck and hurried to the stranded Ford. "I'll take him," he said, and bent to lift Steve in his arms. Viv carried the empty blankets. Beside him in the truck cab, travelling fast, Viv lowered her face till it just touched Stevie's, murmuring and kissing his cheek as he lay against her shoulder. She closed her eyes tightly, but tears sluiced from them, wetting his cheek and hair. She held him tight, swaying slightly to rock him.

At the emergency room they hurried Steve onto a trolley and into surgery. As she followed him through the hall she saw Scott standing at the admission desk, answering the questions of a starchy nurse behind it. She signed the papers they brought her to sign, and waited on the maple bench outside surgery. When the halls were filled with bustle and clinking at dinner time, a nurse brought her a plate of food. She ate it. When the lights lowered, and the sounds quieted down to stray calls, and an occasional hurry of footsteps, a quiet shutting of a door, she dozed a little, upright, with her chin sunk to her chest.

In the night, the doctor came out of Steve's room and sat down beside her, his mask dangling from his neck, to tell her there was nothing more they could do. The appendix had burst, infection had spread everywhere. He set a chair for her beside Steve where he lay small and sturdy in the long bed. Through the Eisenglass window of the oxygen tent she could see him drawing breath solemnly, as if it was his job, till towards dawn, his breaths came slower and slower, and then after a long sigh, quit.

She sat there, her head bent to the tent, quiet, till the nurse returned, and then the doctor, who hoisted the tent, straightened Steve's soft arms out on either side of his body, and pressed one of the small hands firmly down into the dark gray blanket. He walked Viv down the hall to where Scott waited for her. The nurse back of the desk, added a short note to the set of papers. "The body will arrive at Lakeport Funeral Home by afternoon, around four," she said, looking at Scott.

Outside the night seemed quiet and timeless. Scott tucked the blanket and pillow into Viv's side of the cab, to cushion it. "I..." She shook her head, and stopped trying to say anything, only watching the unbroken dark through the windshield. She nodded asleep, and woke and watched. A truck met them, hurrying from the opposite direction. Both trucks slowed to maneuver past each other on the sharp curve.

"That was Charlie," Scott said levelly.

"Yes," Viv answered.

The sun was about ready to come up when they turned into the Hinkley place. The oak tree loomed above the house and quiet yard; the barn looked closed and narrow. Beside it, the flivver stood where it always stood; the tires were fine. Vivian's heart gave a jolting thump. Her mind skittered over the thought that maybe it all hadn't happened that everything was still all right, then corrected itself to reality. "Charlie must have fixed the tire," Scott said.

Vivian shook her head. "He was busy."

At her harsh tone, Scott turned quickly to glance at her. Her expression was set, impassive.

Scott pulled up to the gate and got the suitcase she had packed for Steve down from the truck for her. She took it and stood holding it in front of her with both hands.

"Thanks," she said.

"Isn't there something I can do? Please let me."

"No," she said. "I can't even thank you for what you've done."

"No need. I'll look in later."

The house was perfectly quiet. Nothing called her—or sent her a next cue. She stood in the middle of the kitchen looking around as though she were in a strange place, her thoughts moving slowly like the shadows of big clouds: "It doesn't matter to anybody whether I'm here or not."

Steve's red wagon was near the door to the porch. She imagined him seated there, looking back over his shoulder to see if she was coming, as he always did. I'll never see him do that again, she thought. A black cloud slowed and covered her mind.

She took the pallet and bedding off Izzy's narrow bed and lugged it out to the Ford, collected a few things from her dresser and the bathroom and kitchen and loaded them into the back seat. She stopped at the end of the driveway, her destination still undecided, then turned south uncertainly, slowing when she reached the Hafner place. Liz always kept an emergency key to Neilson's summer cottage set in the midst of a young prune orchard next to them. It was vacant this year because their boy had caught polio, and needed treatments in town. Neilson would let her stay just to have it occupied during the summer when there were strangers around. She pulled over, almost stopped, then speeded up at the last minute, and passed by.

The crossroads was just a little beyond; one branch running uphill through brush and scrub oak to vineyards at the top, and to the left a single lane, used so little the ruts were covered over with flattened pale gold grass. It went down to the creek, and the old Rincon schoolhouse. Where it curved around the hill under a thick canopy of live oaks, it was plated with their shiny, bleached-tan leaves the size of quarters. She had forgotten about that road, though she passed it often. It was a road she knew by foot, rather than from driving it. She could feel the slidy, prickly leaves on bare feet, the tough feet of an eight year old late for school. Twigs scratched across the Ford's top as she wound down through the leafy tunnel. At the bottom, the car spurted out of the shadow for a short sunny run through level dry grass to a shallow creek crossing.

She stopped at its edge. There was no reassuring water-darkened tracks coming out the other side, it was dry, unmarked—it looked all right, but she couldn't judge its depth. She paused a moment listening. The sounds were different here; birds sang at more length. She could hear the stirring of the grass when a breeze passed. It pleased her. She lowered the breast of the flivver into the water gingerly.

On the other side of the creek, in a level opening edged by tall white-oaks, stood the old red school house, abandoned since the central school was built in town and busses started hauling kids to it. She went around back, looking for an unlatched window. The long handled iron pump on the raised back porch stood almost as tall as she did. She remembered how the pump used to sigh when she hung all her weight on the handle, and the handle would go down slowly but never produced any water for her. A new galvanized bucket hung on its spout now. The school still got a little use for meetings, and as a polling place. Its red paint was newer than she remembered. There was a sign posted against trespassers, a formality for outsiders, she felt, not her: she had learned to read here.

Only dry groans and wheezes resulted when she tried the pump, though she kept at it till her hair loosened in a frazzle. Then she took the new bucket to the creek to fill it in the pebbly shallows and stood a long while watching the shadows of fallen leaves dipping and gliding over the pebbles. After awhile she let the bucket fill and lugged it back to pour the water into the pump's neck to prime it, though she didn't remember when she had learned to do that. The pump produced its first bucketful with a shriek, and after the second gurgled a little and offered resistance on the handle, spat a few intermittent jets, and finally began to pour forth a heavy stream. She stopped to rest and look about.

Dapples of shade from the tall oaks shifted on the porch floor which stood scarcely higher than the sun-dried grass. The plank boards over the windows had turned soft silver and shrunk away from the nails. In the stillness she could hear the creek murmuring, a bluejay screeching. Grasshoppers whirred up out of the golden grass and fell back.

With the tire iron from the Ford's tool box she pried the plank off the window next to the porch door. As she had seen her father do, she wrapped her hand in layers of her jacket and, working carefully, broke the glass with the iron and lifted it out.

There stood the desks in rows, graduating from small ones in front to the tall row against the back wall for eighth graders who sometimes had been nearly men. She couldn't remember any of the faces from that time, she couldn't remember what it had been like to be at one of those desks. That was before Charlie or any of the things she now thought of as her life. Only the sunny smells of chalk dust and pine boards seemed familiar.

She climbed in the window, unbolted the door, then as if from habit, went straight to the cloak room on the east side. The narrow closet had a shelf for lunches and books running high up on all its walls. Strong hooks were screwed into its under side from which heavy winter coats had hung like bodies above the pairs of rubber boots and galoshes. She imagined the old aroma of apples, stale bread and wet wool still pervading it. High up, a dim steely light lay outside the clerestory window. The cloak room seemed like a narrow burrow that no one would ever uncover.

She hauled Izzy's cot mattress into it, and made her bed neatly, though she was so tired that the light bedclothes seemed weighted and clinging, making every move hard work. She undressed and crawled into the bed, pulling the covers up over her ears, so she wouldn't have to hear. Darkly, she saw again Steve's little body outlined in their bedroom doorway and heard his cry for help. If she had gathered him up right then, and Charlie had driven them to the hospital so she could hold him and cushion him against any jolts, maybe it would have saved him. Maybe if she had taken him in the morning when she first noticed he was quieter than usual, or if she hadn't wasted time looking for Charlie, it would have made the difference. Again she heard Steve's last long sigh, and then the stillness. She edged over on the pallet so there was room for his body beside her in the curve of hers, and do-nothing tears leaked from the corners of her eyes. As sleep finally was taking her, its forgetfulness, and comfort seemed to her like secret, guilty things.

Chapter 21

When Viv got to Lakeport the next morning Charlie's truck was already parked in front of the funeral parlor. She set the flivver's emergency brake hard though the street was quite level. The mortuary had been made to look like a mansion, with half-round white pillars set into the cement on each side of the door. Julian Keynes, the undertaker opened the door himself when she rang, and held a chair out for her in front of his desk, beside Charlie's. His moves were swift and graceful, so it was hard to remember exactly how he did what he did. He was dressed in a suit of fine dark cloth and a white shirt, and kept his jacket on, and though it was warming up already, he still looked comfortable, easy and everyday. He kept the springiness of his step down most of the time, like an athlete being careful around cripples. Charlie had a folder full of glossy pictures of caskets in his lap and after Viv was seated and was looking up at him after the barest glance at Charlie, Mr. Keynes went on telling them the choices they had. On the wall behind him, framed pictures showed further possibilities, among them, a child's casket, white and pretty. A real sample made of dark wood, deeply padded, and with a fresh pillow, stood by the window, looking all set for somebody's nap.

Mr. Keynes kept his full baritone voice soft and slow, but he was in charge every minute, like the chairman of the meeting. Charlie and Viv sat looking down at the pictures while he talked, insulated by their misery. Finally, Keynes tossed his pencil to the desk in good-natured gesture of defeat, and said excuse me a moment, as he went into a back room.

Charlie turned on Vivian instantly. "Where did you go!" he demanded his voice crisp and angry, and his head drawn back away from her, stiffening his neck.

Mr. Keynes came back into the room with another big card, showing a single, simple box in the center of its big lettered text. This was the bottom of the line, what it almost always came down to. All of this beautiful merchandise, with only a handful of families in the whole county who could afford anything beyond the pine box. Before he could show them, Charlie said abruptly in a half-choked voice, "Where is my son, I want to see him."

"Yes, of course," Mr. Keynes said, in an understanding voice. "Of course—early tomorrow, by ten or—let's just get the funeral arrangements finished and out of the way."

"Excuse me," Viv murmured, after they had chosen the pine casket. She slipped out of her chair and the door while Charlie signed papers. By the time he had finished the arrangements and got out to the sidewalk, there wasn't a sign of her anywhere. He drove with his hands together at the top of the wheel, and his head lowered so he could just see over it. If somebody waved at him, even nodded, he would hit them. Beneath this thin skim of talk in his mind and his grievance at the way Viv was acting, what really occupied him was the yearning to get Stevie in his arms and hold on to him. Just for a while.

From the road, he could see that the flivver wasn't in the yard, which was about what he expected, anyway. He'd have to go asking the neighbors if they knew where his wife was. The bile in his throat diverted him from his sorrow. He sat idle, staring down at the splintered floor boards of the truck.

He heard the sound of footsteps slipping on the loose gravel of the driveway, and looked up quickly, hopeful and hostile, but it was

Kate, not Viv, a little out of breath from walking fast. "Oh, Charlie," she said, "I just heard about Stevie." She came over to the truck, her face ashy and distressed. "Are you all right?" she asked. She grasped the top of the door, and held on to it gently, as if it were his arm, "How's Vivian doing?"

"I don't know. I'm looking for her, myself," Charlie said. "I was going to ask you if you knew where she was, by any chance."

"What do you mean, Charlie? Didn't she come back with you?"

"They left the hospital before I got there last night. She stopped here to take the Ford off somewhere." His voice dried as he said this, "and she showed up all right at the undertaker's this morning, but now she's gone again. I'd hoped she was with you."

Kate blinked, and didn't ask the questions this information raised, but stuck to Charlie's question. "I just don't know who she'd go to, Charlie, except me."

Charlie nodded. "Here, Kate, get in and let me drop you home." he said. They rode the short distance in silence. "If you see Viv before I do," he said as he let her out at her door, "please tell her I want her to come home." His lips pressed together in a prim line, but his quick glance at her was imploring. Then he felt so sheepish he looked down and revved the engine a couple of times to get away.

He turned south driving without aim, braking to a stop when he got to the Neilson place, till he saw there were no recent tread marks beyond the padlocked gate. At the crossroad he looked up the hill speculatively, but there was nobody up there Viv was particularly friendly with, except that wood cutter camped at Colson's. She couldn't very well be sharing his tent. Surely all the women in his family couldn't be just waiting to hook up with tramps of one sort or another. He'd be damned if he was going up there to politely ask him where Viv was. He didn't know what he expected to find by riding up and down the gulch in the dusk; Viv with another flat, or stumbling along the road, lost? It was ridiculous, he'd be better off in bed. He felt drained and aching, and he didn't see how he was going to get through the days ahead. He clung to his grievances till he reached his own driveway again, but as he turned into its ruts and headed toward the house, dim white in the dusk gathering under the oak tree, there was nothing he could do but let his thoughts sink down at their own rate into the cold dark of bereavement.

Chapter 22

Scott cut the sputtering engine and let the saw whir to a stop. It wasn't quitting time yet, but he was thinking more about Viv than about his work and that was no way to handle a buzz saw. He roped the tarp down over the tools and took off for home, though it was only four o'clock and it would be light past eight. Maybe he could stop in on the way to see how she was, and if there was anything he could do. Though the wheel seemed to pull in his hands at her driveway, he went by it. He might be making trouble, and Viv didn't need any more. There was no flivver in the yard, and no truck either. The place had an exposed, empty look. He wondered if Vivian could have left, and where she would go, and if she had gone, who was taking care of the rabbits? The answer to that was nobody, if he knew Charlie, which of course he didn't. He wheeled at the old winery turnout, and went back. The wire pens were still there back of the barn, and in each of them the rabbits were huddled together in one corner, silent, till he got close to them. That set them scrabbling frantically and crowding even tighter together. Tufts of fur stuck up from the living heaps like trash. Their dishes were empty and dry, He filled their fountains, and plunged his arm into the furry mass to break it up so everybody would have a chance to drink; it was like trying to mold mud. He filled their dishes with food pellets, but it was water they were dying for.

He let them drink while he tried to figure out what the situation was, and what he should do. There were plenty of objections to his interfering, but he couldn't just let them die. He moved the truck up till be could slide the hutches into the back, four of them, one after the other, with the rabbits sliding along the bottom, and rearing against the wires in fright. It would take at least two trips to move them all.

Daniel Colson was coming out of the barn when he arrived with the rabbits. When Scott told him about the death of the child, his face winced as though he had been hit. "Well, at least we can feed the rabbits," he said.

Gyp came up from the gully, his trot breaking into a run as he spotted the wire hutches seething with fur, and when he got near them he raised a yapping blare of protest.

"Let them alone, Gyp," Colson commanded, and when he didn't stop, bent down to shove him away. "That's enough now." Gyp sat down a little way off, staring at the cages and began a series of half smothered barks, nipped off whenever Colson turned to stop him, resumed when he dared.

Pa made Gyp come up to the house with him when it was time for dinner, but as soon as he had gobbled up his bowl of food, he turned down to the barn again, and settled in barking hollowly at intervals, standing uneasy guard in between. He was still unappeased when Beulah came down to get him for the night.

"What's the matter with you, you've seen rabbits before, you crazy dog. Let them alone."

"Uff, uff." His voice was hoarse and he sounded dead weary but unrelenting. His stomach contracted with each slow bark, as if the thought of rabbits made him retch. He wouldn't obey, though he understood perfectly, and looked guilty about it. Jess came to help her with a length of rope through his dog collar to haul him up the hill. Gyp braced his legs so he slid and strained his neck back toward the hutches, the white of one eye flashing oddly as he choked.

Jess tied him to the ring on his dog house, but when it got dark, he chewed the rope through, and went back. They could hear him off and on through the night his bark growing weaker and weaker.

He seemed worn out when he came up for his breakfast. Beulah's face looked all pinched up and so pitiful he went to a corner and lay down facing them with his paws stretched out in front and his chin flat on them, rolling his eyes up at her. Pa had told Beulah about Stevie, and though she hadn't seen him much, she remembered him perfectly. He was beautiful, like a carved angel she'd seen in a magazine, and besides, the thought of your baby dying like that just about made her knees buckle. She could tell Pa felt bad too, and even Jess, who didn't know the child.

As soon as Gyp's food took hold, he got restless, and nosed the screen door open to trot down the hill to the rabbits, and started up again. Scott came out of his tent and was watching Gyp speculatively. He didn't try to talk Gyp out of it, but tossed a tiny pebble at him. Pa came down to join Scott.

"I don't think he's ever going to give up on this."

"Maybe not. He might get used to them in time, but it might be simpler for me to move the tent somewhere else and take them with me till Mrs. Norton can handle them."

"Why not just take them up to Jess's place, if you wouldn't mind moving them again. Ernie can feed them, and maybe you could look out for them some. Better yet, maybe she would be willing to move in up there, and let Ernie come back to the bunkhouse, which he's pining to do." Scott said he'd move the rabbits then, whatever happened later.

When he and Beulah drove in for their regular shopping trip at the Wilke's vegetable patch, he looked for any signs of change at the Hinkley place as they passed it, but it looked as forsaken as before.

Kate Wilkes started to shake her head, when he asked if she knew where Vivian was, then said, "Wait, she might shelter in the old schoolhouse. I don't know why I didn't think of it when Charlie was looking for her yesterday."

"Where is it?" Scott asked.

"It's just down from the crossroads. Beulah can show you, can't you, Beulah, though I imagine you were too young to go to school there. I know Vivian did." She studied Scott, wondering what he could do.

"Well, at least, I can tell her where her rabbits are."

"If you find her, give her these, will you?" She bagged some corn and Blue Lake beans, a lemon cucumber, apricots, and made up a triangle paper packet of blackberries.

Vivian sat at the back of the schoolroom at one of the desks for the big boys. The room was warm and still, filled with a dusky brown light streaked with shafts of sunlight from the cracks in the window boarding. She was not doing anything with her hands; she could not have said where her thoughts were. It was restful, not like the nights, sleepless while she schemed over and over what she could have done to save him.

He had been so pleased when the toy bat he swung even ticked the ball she tossed him. She wished he could have grown to really smack it into the stands and round the bases happy and grinning, as Charlie used to do. The sober attention Stevie gave the animals would have been love and steadiness later on, at the same time as he'd always see the fun in things. Once he'd gotten big enough to make his decisions, Stevie would have been really independent, he'd have done what he set out to do, if he'd just had his chance. He'd have been there for his wife and his children with every drop of blood in his body, if he'd got to be a man. And the world wouldn't have been roughed up by his passing through it. It would have benefited every step of the way. She sort of rocked in her chair thinking of the respect and love Stevie had coming to him that he'd never have a chance to collect. Well, he'd known how much she loved him and counted on him, and what fun and comfort she'd had from him. She was glad they'd had such a good time together, but a mother was just a start to what life was going to hand you. Just a little start. You pretty much did the rest for yourself, and she knew Stevie would have done fine, if he could have had his chance.

She surfaced slowly as the sound of the truck got closer, and slipped into the cloak room when it stopped in front. She could hear a mixture of footsteps alongside the room, and a man's voice accompanying them, then a knock at the back door.

"Hoo hoo, Mrs. Norton, we've brought you something from Kate." She had to open the door to Beulah, there was no way to not do that.

She took the sack from Beulah, but looked disconcerted. Scott explained, "She wanted to tell you we had taken the rabbits up to Jess Sooter's place where they could be fed and watered. I thought you wouldn't mind if you knew they were being tended."

Beulah broke in, "They settled down fine, but Pa says he wished you could come live there yourself, and let Ernie get back to the bunkhouse."

"That's very generous. I appreciate it but 1 can't accept it. I'm glad they were rescued, but I guess I'm through with rabbits."

"Don't say that," Scott said, "What am I going to eat, then?" The raspy shout of a jay rang over and over in the willows.

Viv looked very sober, and said, "I haven't thought about arrangements. I guess the real question is 'What am I going to eat?'" she said finally. "I'd forgotten the rabbits are going to have to make my living from now on." She turned to Beulah "We'll pay you good rent once we settle in, Beulah. I never could raise all the rabbits people wanted to buy, let alone the butcher and the grocery store. I'll come this afternoon, as soon as I can pick up some of my clothes and things."

"Well, that's good," Beulah said, smiling her brilliant gap-toothed smile.

Scott asked, "Can I take something up there for you, now? I've got the truck empty." Viv started to say that wouldn't be necessary, then turned the shake of her head into a nod, her eyes looked dark with distress. He followed her into the cloakroom where she bundled the clothes and blanket into a box for him to take, and gathered Izzy's pallet in her arms to take out to the flivver herself.

She was in front of the Hinkley house hauling it out of the back seat when Charlie pulled into the yard. He killed the engine when he had pulled up beside her, and looking down from the cab asked, "You back?"

"I came to return Iz's bed and pick up some clothes."

"Just passing through, huh?" He stared straight ahead through the windshield at nothing a while, then turned to her again and asked coldly, "What about me?"

"I don't know about you, Charlie, except that I don't want to ever see you again." She tightened the roll of mattress, and headed for the house with it. He jumped down from the truck and took the mattress away from her, pushed the side door open with it and dumped it down on the springs in Izzy's empty room. He followed her past Stevie's room, where the crib stood bare of blankets, with its side rail down. She stuffed a pillow case with her belongings, and went to the kitchen, garnered a paper bag of utensils, and then started across the yard. He watched her from the door, idle and dispassionate, then suddenly strode out to her and grabbed her arm. "Don't you ignore me, God dammit. You act like I killed him. Christ, Vivian, everything can't be my fault."

"I never said it was," she said wearily. "We got him to the hospital just as quick as you could have." He shook her arm.

"Then what do you think you're doing."

She held onto the case, and jerked her arm free. "Let me alone, I'm going."

He released her, giving her elbow a shove so that she stumbled slightly. "Yeah, I'll let you alone, if that's what you want. I certainly will."

She drove out the driveway fast, the flivver jouncing high, and skittering on the ruts. She had to get out of sight of Charlie; she didn't want to see him or hear him or think about him, but the main thing was she didn't want him to be able to see her—she felt so ashamed.

When she swung out onto the main road, she turned her face and hunched a shoulder to her cheek to wipe away the tears sliding down it. She could see Charlie, one hand on the handle of the truck door, the other propped against the rim of the windshield staring at the ground.

Chapter 23

Coming from the north as they did when they went into town before they stopped for vegetables, Beulah could look right down on the whole spread of the Wilkes's—truck garden and the orchards behind it from ten or twelve feet above when they rounded the hill in Mr. Scott's truck. She could see down the rows of vegetables, how some were staked up or strung along stiff round wires, and some just left to crawl along the ground because that was the way they did best. The ground was patterned dark and light, where some had been fresh watered, but not all.

It looked different from the last time they came this way. The asparagus had shot up pretty as ferns, but so wiry you couldn't eat it. The lemon cucumber vines drying out and losing their leaves looked like big round nests with gold eggs. They wouldn't be so hard to find among their leaves, any more, but she guessed they'd probably be pithy by now.

Kate looked over her shoulder when they drove up to the stand. She was laying out butternut squash on the table, one by one. They looked like babies, even the right color, almost. That was the first thing Beulah bought. The big one she chose almost filled her paper bag, so when Kate finished putting out the rest, she said she'd carry it so Beulah would have room for other things. She cradled it in the crook of her arm while Beulah picked out her other vegetables. Kate always told her which were best, and which were past their peak. That was the way Beulah had got so she could talk to Kate easier than to most. She enjoyed it so much she would keep on picking out vegetables till sometimes Kate would laugh and say maybe they should go around again and put back some of the perishables till her next visit.

Hot weather or not, what she was hungry for right now was a good beef stew, so after the salad stuff, Beulah got her turnips and parsnips and parsley for it. She had enough carrots and potatoes and onions on hand already—Ernie grew those. Some people turned up their noses at turnips, but she knew they were what made all the rest of a stew taste so good. At home everybody had a specialty they cooked, like Ernie and his fried mush. Stew was hers, and the secret was turnips.

"Is Vivian getting along all right at the new place?" Kate asked, as they mosied along the greens table. "Do you see much of her?"

"Some," Beulah answered thoughtfully, "When Jess wants me to get something he left up at the place, like yesterday his pruning shears." What she felt was that Mrs. Norton needed a lot of let-alone, so she tried not to bother her unless she had to. "The rabbit pens are fixed up dandy now. Mr. Scott did that, then she did some on her own. He eats a lot of rabbit. He says they're real good." She shook her head in wonder. "He put up a big 'Rabbits' sign for her, and people come to buy them. She says she makes so much money off rabbits she doesn't have to eat them herself any more."

Scott met them at the table. "I think I'll go check the berry patch for strays, if I may, Mrs. Wilkes. There's always a few left." When he disappeared down the bank to where the berries were Kate asked Beulah how she had been feeling lately. Beulah told her, and Kate, judging from her own five pregnancies, concluded she was doing fine. On a strapping young woman like Beulah, a baby wouldn't show much, even in the sixth month.

Scott foraged among the leaves for the last raspberries. Pickers always missed some; you could count on it. It was a peaceful work, the occasional rewards seemed precious. From nowhere, as simply as the sun coming out, the realization came over him: he wanted to marry Viv. He wanted to marry Viv. His long conviction that he wouldn't marry again after his wife's painful death simply disappeared. He wanted to marry Vivian, and there was absolutely nothing he could do about it now. Vivian would need time, and he would have to give it to her.

He heard a car slow down and turn into the driveway; he climbed part way up the bank to see who it was. Two women and a child in a new Model A. He'd seen them before, in town, now and then.

Kate watched Ernestine Popple trundle her green roadster carefully into the shade on the far side of the barn. She and her sister Bernice, both rather large women, unloaded themselves deliberately. Each kept hold of one of the child's hands as they came toward the stand. Edison, who was waist-high already, naturally wanted to run, so they made jerky progress, Ernestine holding back because of her new kid Cuban heeled pumps.

They reached the stand shoes unscathed and she relaxed and smiled broadly, then. "Good morning, Kate. Have you got something new for us, today? The peas last week were perfect." Bernice smiled too, and nodded to indicate her sister spoke for both of them.

"Well," Kate said, "there's more new squash, and some nice honeydews. That's about it."

Selecting lettuce, they moved near to Beulah at the table. Ernestine turned her face to one side to look sharply at her through one eye. "Oh, hello, it's Beulah Colson, isn't it. I hear Vivian Norton moved in next to your place. I bet that was a surprise."

Beulah shied slightly, and blinked. Her voice sounded relieved when she found the answer, "No, it wasn't. We asked her."

"I mean, it was a surprise that she would leave her husband like she did." Mrs. Popple looked around at her sister and Kate, to assure herself of a reasonable audience.

"I should say so," Bernice said.

"With a child fresh in the ground, you'd think she'd wait a decent interval. Do you remember Bernice, they didn't even leave the graveyard together."

"Yes, I do," Bernice affirmed. "It struck me then."

Kate was conscious then that the squash she was carrying looked like a baby in her arms, and shifted it so it didn't. She generally tried to steer clear of talking about Stevie's funeral with Beulah, because she had noticed Beulah still seemed at a loss, upset and confused about it, but these two were going to talk about it, and there was no stopping them; she could tell that.

"Of course, I feel terribly sorry for her. It's always so sad to see a grave that size." Bernice blew her nose and turned around to see her nephew safely eating peas out of a pod. Sorrow was gathering in Beulah's soft, long face, making it look puckered.

Bernice went on. "He seemed like such a sturdy little boy," she sniffed jerkily, like sobbing backwards, and blotted her eyes alternately with a folded handkerchief, "even in his coffin."

"Like a little dead angel," Beulah said, her voice small and wondering.

"I just can't understand how any mother could let a child get that sick without taking care of it." Mrs. Popple shook her bead victoriously from side to side, like a dog with a rope in his teeth.

"You know Ernestine," her sister argued, "I think she did all she could to get it to the hospital. You know those old flivvers." She folded her arms across her chest. "Where was her husband when she needed him, that a strange man had to take her dying baby to the hospital? And who paid the bill? That's what I want to know." Bernice's husband had gone hunting shortly after their marriage, and had got shot. She still resented it.

Scott came around the end of the house with a loaded bag in one hand and a tray of stained wooden berry boxes in the other. He showed them to Beulah. "This is the last of the berries for now."

"Raspberries, my favorite," Beulah said. "Mrs. Norton said that's her favorite too. We can take her some."

Scott assayed her collection of bags. "If you've got everything you want, I'll get the truck and pick you up here. O.K.?" They paid. Kate walked with Scott as far as the barn, to get fresh water in the sprinkling can.

"That's the one!" Ernestine hissed, tipping her head sideways toward Bernice. The whisper, though it was loud enough to be heard a good ways, somehow exempted her from considering Beulah present. "Letty told me it was the tramp wood-cutter that goes around with a whole load of saws in the back of his truck. She says he's camped on the creek at Colson's ranch, right by the barn, as if he belonged."

"Well, he's certainly handsome, all right," Bernice said. "Wouldn't you know."

"If you like that burly, auburn type. I think there's something brutish about it, myself. He was seen coming out of the Norton's place the very day after the baby died." She faced her sister squarely, to be sure this sank in. Bernice looked bland.

Mrs. Popple went on, "Now I'm reminded of it, Letty said something last year about him, the first time we saw him from the road, with a buzz saw howling so you couldn't hear your own engine. She says he was involved in that IWW trouble up in the timber country, some years ago. She closed her eyes and licked her lips, consulting an inner oracle. "He was one of the main ones in the news. A whole bunch were arrested. Somebody was killed, I think, but I guess he didn't do it, at least he didn't get convicted."

Bernice nodded, her expression mild to excuse her sisters' failure of memory. "I didn't make a connection till now, either," she contributed, "but there was a fight over a girl at the last Lakeport dance, and one of the men in it was described as a big, red-headed man just like him."

Ernestine nodded, soberly accepting Bernice's deference. "Like as not it was the same man. Can you believe a married woman, a mother, acting like that?"

Beulah looked from one to the other as confused as if they spoke in tongues. When Scott stopped for her, she climbed into the cab and sat looking stricken.

"What's the matter?" Scott asked, after the truck straightened out and he glimpsed her posture. He slowed and looked at her closely. "Do you feel ill?"

She shook her head, pressing her lips together to keep back tears. "They talk like everybody is bad."

"Oh," Scott said, relieved. "I wouldn't let that worry me if I were you, Mrs. Sooter. That's the way some people are."

Kate had seen the truck nearly come to a stop, and the way Scott turned his head to look at Beulah. She returned to the stand, her gentle face stern.

"You'll have to finish quickly, ladies, I have to start supper," she said in a level, final voice, and began covering what was left of the produce. When the women had loaded their bag into the back of the car, and had the child safely between them in front, Ernestine had a new insight.

"You did hear that the Norton girl ran off, didn't you? 'Eloped,' they said, though 'eloped' covers a lot of territory if you ask me. With a mother like that, it doesn't come as much surprise, does it."

"No, indeed it doesn't," Bernice answered, staying in line. She lifted Edison, whose knee was interfering with the shift stick, onto her lap where he settled against her comfortably.

"It looked to me like that simple-minded Colson girl was pregnant," she essayed.

"You think so?" Ernestine turned eyes wide with surprise and speculation on her sister. "My God," she said hoarsely. "What next."

Beulah stopped off at Jess's old place to give Vivian the mail they had picked up for her, while Scott went on with the truck. There was one of Isobel's letters in it so she didn't want it to wait. She found Vivian in the barn, fixing up some small single hutches with straw and water pans.

"This is going to be my isolation ward," she told Beulah. She sorted through the little bundle—the *Kelseyville Sun*, a flyer for the Lakeport movie house, and Izzy's letter. She dropped the rest and tore that open. Beulah said she or Mr. Scott would bring her vegetables as soon as they got unloaded, and left her to read it.

When Scott, loaded with bags of vegetables, approached the open barn door, he could hear her voice going on, quietly. She was putting a puny rabbit into the new quarters. "What do you think, Stevie? Do you think he'll settle in and get to like it?" He saw her stroking the petrified creature. "Izzy's letter says she's signed up for high school where she is, so that's a relief. She says she misses you, and she's afraid you'll be a big boy by the time she gets back for a visit."

She heard Scott trying to back out quietly with his load of vegetables. She turned to him, "Come in," she said, "and don't worry, I'm not crazy. I just do that because I like to," she said simply.

"I can see how you would," Scott said. He turned his back, looking for a place to put the sacks down, but mostly to give her time. He put them down by the feed bin, and started to set apples from one of the bags in a row, perfect golden yellow with their striped pink cheeks facing all the same way, like fat soldiers. "Kate said these were your favorite for pies," he said, lining then up carefully. When the bag was empty, he looked at her. "I have to head back to Washington, tomorrow. I'll be back next May, so I just want to say goodbye till then."

Viv disengaged herself from the rabbits, and looked at him quietly. "I never seem to be able to thank you, but I do."

"No need for you to, ever." They stood peacefully together a moment. "Well then, 'til Spring," he said.

It was still hot after supper, in the kitchen especially. Beulah stepped outside for some air, and then began to think how nice it would be to have a swim to cool off. This time of year the barranco was dry as a bone, but the mill pond on Kelsey creek didn't even get low because of the dam. It was an easy walk though she noticed her stride was shorter than when she last lit out to get somewhere fast. She guessed that was because her belly was so big.

The pond was deep green, and beautiful with the big oaks on the mill side and the steep rocky bank on the other side. She swam across and back once with her head out, so as to keep the curl in her hair, then decided she would get under altogether, because that was the way to really get all the tired out of you at the end of a day.

Going home she went a little out of her way so she could set out into the alfalfa field. This was her favorite place of all at dusk, when she could let her eyes ride along the rim of hills in the strip of silver light that stayed on last of all there between the dark hills and the darkening sky. It cleared her mind so she hardly knew what she was thinking about till she felt the pull of sorrow in her throat, like a cord was been pulled tighter and tighter.

She was thinking about Stevie, wondering if where he was was dark now, and where he would go next, and whether there was someone he knew there to take care of him.

A thump in her belly jolted her out of her reverie. She leaned back on her arms, and regarded her rounded middle. Thump, again it came, and in the dusky light she could see the sudden bulge as though a sharp little elbow or knee came near to bursting through. She watched with wonderment. There went a smoother bulge right over the top, in a long, gliding swoop, like a kid down a haystack. She lost her breath watching.

Could it be time for the baby, she wondered, even though the doctor said it wasn't due for a while yet. She had tried to figure out when it would be, but she had never kept track much, and she got mixed up reckoning this, and adding up that. Besides, it didn't really matter what she figured out, or what the doctor predicted. The baby would come in its own sweet time.

She listened to the wild things settling for the night in the thicket of elderberry and cottonwoods strung with ropes of wild grapevine that bordered the barranco. She could hear birds hopping in the tangle, and frogs in the bushes sawing away at the same notes over and over, and a couple of squirrels making a last dark commotion in the trees. The mystery of it with the dusk so thick around her smothered her, and she was beginning to get the feeling she was lost somewhere she'd never been, the way she used to. Then the first star pricked through, then others, showing a spangle that raised the sky back up to a high arch again, and she could see she was right at the center.

Chapter 24

Irv couldn't believe how fast it had happened. Last week Bill and he were talking, kind of random, Bill scheming about getting out of Lake County, and him trying to figure out how to stay in it. He didn't say anything about his real dream, because that was about Beth, and Beth was Bill's girl, hands-off. Next thing he knew Bill was saying good bye to his folks, and they kept saying they were glad he finally got the good break he deserved, but they looked so sad it was pitiful. Umps cried all the time. Bill said he'd be back the first time he got a vacation and that he'd miss everybody like the very deuce.

The whole time, Bill hadn't said a word about Beth, except, after he took her out the last night before he left, he said that it was too bad there weren't more opportunities for a girl like Beth in Lake County, sort of like it was a humanitarian concern and she was some interesting statistic. It galled him that Bill would walk out on a girl like Beth without any more thought than those platitudes. He kept wondering how it made Beth feel to be left cold like that, and he knew the answer was "terrible".

He felt discarded himself, as if he knew in his bones that he and Bill would never be the same again. They had weathered a lot of changes since he was fifteen and the strong man of the bunch and Bill, thirteen, was the runt. Then Bill got ahead of him in school, but he got that job at the Country Club after school and was the worldly wised-up one. Finally Bill shot up a lot taller than him—but none of that had made any difference.

Well, they weren't kids anymore. And now things were different in more ways than one, but still, he'd no more make a move toward Beth than if she was Bill's wife. In a funny way, that had backfired, because it eliminated all the flirty stuff that he was no good at anyway. It only made him love Beth more, because she was just as she really was, with him. She acted different with Bill—fancier, and more careful of what she said and did. He liked the straight way she was with him better.

It made him sore when Bill would refer to Beth as "Susie" when she wasn't there, as if he wanted to belittle her, sort of. Resentment swelled inside him. He didn't like feeling critical of Bill, it went against all the years they'd been buddies. He saw now that they'd been going in opposite directions all summer long, though he'd never faced it before. Like the way Bill looked down on the fruit tramps. Bill always looked at them from the boss's side, he never once put himself in their shoes. That was it, sort of. Bill was on his way to be the boss himself, and was impatient of any other attitude. It really was "Goodbye, Bill," as if he could see Bill vanishing, like a plane you watched dwindle in the distance till it wasn't there at all.

Then little by little it dawned on him that the whole summer he'd been so careful to lay off of Beth because of Bill, Bill hadn't really wanted her to be his girl, even though she was.

Memories and hopes he'd held down so long it was a habit shot up like balloons released under water: pictures in his mind of him and Beth together, lying side by side in the last sunny spot of sand by the lake, or linking arms after the parade. It was the memory of how they felt dancing together that flooded over everything else.

There was a Lakeport dance this Saturday. He'd ask her in his own right this time, not pinch hitting for Bill, and this time when they walked down to the water he would kiss her, the way he'd wanted to so much at the dance.

He'd driven the whole way to work without thinking about it, as if the truck knew the way. He turned into the yard at the Oaks, and checked in with the manager right away to make sure he realized Bill wasn't going to be there, and asked him if he should tell the other men in his crew what had happened.

The manager told him to take Bill's crew over, just as Bill had predicted. He could handle that now, easily. Maybe he'd ridden on Bill's coat tails too long. The pressure of the peak of the season was long over. What was left to do mainly took common sense and patience. He was a little scared, and very serious when he explained the job for the day to his men.

Beth opened the door to him herself, Saturday night. He handed her a big yellow rose from Mrs. Winton's bushes. Beth said it matched his hair, and put it up beside his ear to admire it, then fixed it in her own shiny dark hair and turned her head slowly, like a queen, to show him how she looked.

At the dance, much as they tried to avoid breaking up, once in a while she would say she couldn't get out of dancing with some friend. Instead of picking another partner then, he just hung out in a corner of the hall, plans tumbling and reforming in his mind. He would make the Winton's take board money, so he wouldn't be an expense to them, and stay in Lake County as long as there was work, to be near Beth. When he did go back, he could carry some extra work besides his main job, so he could get enough money ahead to ask her to marry him. Then with the two of them working, they would save up for a down payment on a Lake County place, maybe not in the Rincon, but in the big valley nearer the lake. No matter what Bill said about Lake County, some people down there had nice set ups and made good money. Anything was possible if you used you head and were willing to work.

When he cut in again, Beth acted like it was their secret how glad she was to be with him again. The band was sounding more and more dreamy as it got near time to quit. When they launched into

"Let Me Call You Sweetheart" this time, he and Beth danced slower and slower, and then just stopped and kissed till the final cord and trembling crash of the cymbal. She rode home with her head against his shoulder, curled up and silent, so he had to look down from time to time to see if she was asleep, then she would raise up her face to show him she wasn't, and snuggle down against him again. The moon was riding high and silvery, washing everything below with clear pale light. They walked up the path to Beth's door with their arms around each other's waist not saying a word so they wouldn't wake up Frank. A few roses left on the bushes lining the path glimmered like ghosts among the dark leaves. Tree frogs shrilled everywhere. Nothing would ever change, the night promised.

In spite of their cautious steps, the porch creaked loudly. He could hear Frank call, "That you, Babe?" followed by a bump and a scraping sound like he'd run into a piece of heavy furniture, then some curses. Beth pushed the door open. "It's me, Pa," she said. When she turned to look back at Irv over her shoulder as she pushed the door open, he whispered, "We'll go out on the lake tomorrow, O.K.?"

"O.K." she whispered back, and closed the door softly behind her.

Beth handed him a heavy lunch basket when he came to pick her up. He groaned, pretending he could hardly lift it. "This for a family of five?"

"I fixed it while I was hungry," she explained. He had the Winton's Ford truck, this time. She climbed up onto the seat quickly, the full skirt of her pink cotton dress rippling around her pale-tanned legs, and held on to the side of the seat and laughed when the truck got going good on the downhill run to the lake.

The summer businesses and Soda Bay were boarded up already, but the bait shack, still open for fishermen, rented him a small rowboat with an outboard motor on it. The huge shadow from Mt.

Konocti kept the water along the shore glassy and dark, and the immense morning stillness reduced the sound of the little motor to a pulse beat. He steered straight out for the North shore, the boat pulling a quiet wake behind it. A bluish haze of exhaust spread over the dark reflections in the water. Beth was absorbed in watching her fingers dip in and out of the ripples beside the boat. He felt as if he had all the treasure of the world in his care. His joy built like a summer thunderhead. Halfway to the middle of the lake they moved out of the mountain shadow into the dazzle of sunshine. The heat of it surprised them. The steep slopes of the hills on the far shore, bare except for a thin cover of bleached grass, reflected the glare. The motor sounded louder and harried, as though the whole day had got busier. When he squinted up at the sun itself, it looked as though it was drilling through the sky, aimed at them, personally.

"We better get out of the sun pretty quick," he said. "It looks like it wants to kill us." He turned sharp right to round the jut of land that formed the bay, and a whole new vista of the lake spread out before him. He'd never thought about the lake going on any farther than he could see from Soda Bay, but it did, a great stretch of it came into sight with a small island shaded with thick growing pines not very far out.

"Will you look at that?" he said. He could barely believe the luck.

"Perfect. Let's pull up on it and have a swim. My suit's beginning to itch."

He let the engine full out till they neared the island, then cut it to drift into its pebbly shallows. He rolled his pant legs up to his knees and slid into the water to hold the light boat steady for Beth. She peeled her dress off over her head, almost with one motion it seemed to him, and was ready in her black swim suit. The minute she was free of the boat, she dipped in up to her chin, then stood up and lifted water in her cupped hands to wet her face.

It looked so good he did the same thing, since the water came up over his pants anyway. They hauled the boat up on the shore, and stowed the lunch in the shade, and then swam till they cooled off. He lay in the sand, panting, while the sun warmed through the chill on his skin, then much as he hated to move, he had to find a shady spot. Beth strolled after him, toweling the damp ends of her hair. He settled on a deep bed of pine needles under the biggest tree, spread his towel carefully, on hands and knees, and flopped face down on it. When he propped himself on an elbow to see where she had gone, she was right beside him, on her own towel but almost nose to nose with him, so close it made him laugh with surprise. He put a hand under the wet hair on her neck and stretched forward to kiss her. She seemed so accepting and self forgetful that before he even thought about it they'd gone further than he'd hoped to get in a month. He started to struggle with the shoulder straps of her suit, she just sat up straight and still and let him slip them halfway down her arms and then leaned back on her hands so that she was offering her bare breasts to his lips. It was the most beautiful thing he'd ever seen. They sank down together on the sweet smelling pine needles, and he was lost to history, till finally he had to break away to keep from coming, it felt so much like the real thing even though they were just petting. When he looked at Beth, she was lying with her eyes closed, as if she was lost in the same dream as him. As he moved away, she tilted her face toward him again, still with her eyes closed like she was hunting for him in the dark with her lips, beseeching him. Not answering that would seem like taking advantage, somehow, though that was exactly opposite what "taking advantage" usually meant but he was beginning to think that a lot of the things people said were exactly opposite true.

He could feel the alternating stripes of warm and cold of her body as she pulled her wet suit off the rest of the way. As he pushed his own trunks off with his feet, his thick white thighs and calves, ornamented with curly gold hairs, look comic compared to her polished ivory body.

He'd always thought he'd keep really in control of himself with a virgin, slow and gentle. He'd started out that way, alright, and for a minute Beth had hardly moved a muscle, and her thighs were clinched together. But then she let go, and he lost his head, and as for giving Beth any tender guidance, that was a laugh, she was so natural he didn't even have to think of it. It was like when they danced together, nobody had to think about anything.

The prickling of the pine needles, and the scratchy sand didn't begin to get through to him till later. He brushed Beth's back, and could see the curved red marks the long needles had pressed into her pale tan. The pine scent was sharp in the warm air. For a while, he was too happy to think about anything, let alone talk. He just lay looking up through the branches, not feeling guilty for once, since naturally they'd get married, now. Beth was quiet too. He wondered what she was thinking, but there didn't seem to be any way to ask. When he turned his head to look at her, she returned his look with a smile that looked so much like the way he felt that it was as good as an answer.

It was all so confounded wonderful he laughed out loud. It was for Beth, too, he had every reason to believe. Compared to those poor women at the country club he'd been with, well, there wasn't any comparison. This was so different he didn't want to think of it with the same brain, even. He'd make sure Beth never had to regret that she went with him. He would love Beth till the day he died.

He didn't realize he had dropped asleep till he saw Beth had put on her dress, and was setting the lunch out on a little checked cloth she had covered the basket with. Both of their swim suits were spread out nicely to dry. His felt damp and warm as he pulled it on.

The last thing Beth took out of the basket was a bottle of wine. "I brought some of Pa's best. German Dago Red," she said, handing him a glass of it.

"To the bride," he said, and drank. Then he put his glass down, nesting it in the pine needles. "You will marry me, won't you?"

She bent her head a minute, then looked back at him and said, "Yes, I will." When he reached for her hand over the spread-out picnic, she laced her finger with his. He'd never seen her look so quiet and serious before, or so beautiful. He'd never even hoped to be as happy as he was this minute. Ever.

Two fishermen were humped over their poles in a rowboat off shore a couple of hundred yards. They were as still as cut-out cardboard, but they looked like they were leaning forward, listening, expecting. He could hear the sound of a motor boat doing zigzags just beyond the isthmus. Some college kids water skiing one more time before they had to go back to school, likely. The way things stood now, he'd better get back to the city himself, by the end of the week, at the latest, to get fill-in work till Barney's job came through. That didn't leave him much time with Beth, dammit. He thought what it would have been like to have had the whole summer together, but that brought up Bill again. He let that thought go. He'd better worry about what was going to happen, not what hadn't.

He told Beth what he was thinking, about the idea of getting an extra part-time job, a real one, not just the Country Club, so they could get their own place that much sooner. She listened to what he was saying and watched him closely, as though she was a student learning a new language. It made him want to laugh. He sure wished he was as smart about getting work as he sounded. He was just lucky that Barney remembered him and wanted him to work for him. She said maybe she could get on at the Club, herself. She knew how to do a lot of that kind of stuff from working Ma's dinners. But he put the kybosh on that. He certainly wasn't going to have his wife working at the Club. It wouldn't take him long, he assured her. He'd be back for her in no time.

They swam again, and lay in the hot sun to dry, close and quiet in each other's arms, murmuring to each other, sometimes plotting terrible things to happen to the floating fishermen, sometimes lost in feeling.

Irv noticed that the sun, quite suddenly it seemed, was lowering. He jumped to his feet and reached a hand down for Beth. "I've got to get the truck back to Pod," he said. "he has to round up some grape boxes before night."

Beth was quiet on the way back. In the boat, she sat in the prow, a lot of the time with her head on her drawn up knees, and her arms crossed at her ankles, as though her thoughts had taken her far away. In the truck it was too noisy to talk much anyway, but he had the same feeling. When he pulled up opposite her house he turned to take her in his arms. She pushed back into the corner of the seat, and said in a tone that mixed urgency and dismay, "No, wait," and looked at him in a searching almost hostile way. "I'm not going to do it."

He thought she was saying she wasn't going to marry him, and he was sure right away the reason was that she was still thinking about Bill. He knew he couldn't compare to Bill. Still the look baffled him.

"What do you mean?" It was just a cry; he knew what she meant, all right.

"I was going to fool you into thinking the baby was yours." She shook her head, and tears stood in her eyes, but she stayed distant and unsmiling.

"What baby? For God's sake, what are you talking about, Beth?"

"My baby. I'm pregnant, and I thought I could make you think it was yours, but I'm not going to do it."

"Are you serious?" he half stammered. He hated every image that whirled in his head. "Whose is it?" His voice was pinched, as if he was expecting news so terrible he could scarcely bare to ask for it.

"It's Earl's," Beth said flatly. His breath came out so hard when he let it go that it made a syllable. At least it wasn't Bill's baby.

Then when the thought that it was Earl's really reached him, the anger that billowed through him felt as good as gaiety. "That Bastard!" he blustered through a rote of profanity and imprecation, reviving and relieving. "He raped you!"

"No! Yes! No!" Her eyes stayed steady, and cold. "It wasn't rape. I wanted him to."

"Jesus, Beth, how could you." He couldn't believe what she said. That oaf. He slumped in his seat, staring out the windshield.

"I was used to him." Her voice was flat level. It took a moment for Irv's face to react, the way a dynamited building stands up a second before crumbling.

"I couldn't make him stop without Pa's knowing about us, and besides I didn't want to." She shook her head. She looked insistent while she said this, exacting, as though her only interest was to make herself clear.

He felt as though he had been whipped. "On the island, then, that was all fake."

"Oh, I meant to pretend I was virgin, but I quit. I just didn't want to pretend. The rest wasn't fake." She said this as harshly as the rest. She turned away from him and tried to get out, but the truck door stuck. He grabbed her arms and shoved her back in the corner and looked at her. Her eyes were sparking with resentment and defiance as she twisted out of his grip. He dropped his hands, "Jesus, Beth. What am I supposed to do?"

"I don't know," she said.

He got out and walked wearily around the truck to open the door for her. "I don't know either." What he wanted was to find a hole and crawl into it. Beth's face gradually lost its look of agitation and insistence and became sorrowful. He had to look away to keep himself from trying to comfort her. He stared at the ground, and then roused himself briskly. "Well, I'll see you." His voice was strained and civil.

He drove into the Winton driveway holding on to the one thought he could stand, that at least it wasn't Bill's kid, though why that should be such a relief was something he couldn't fathom. That had been his first thought, as Beth told him, and it had thrown him for such a loop, that for a minute he had almost been glad when she said the baby was Earl's.

Pictures of the day on the island with Beth kept intertwining with dark pictures of Earl and her struggling together. He could hear them laughing. He had to figure it all out, but his whole being shied away from it like a horse he couldn't handle. About all he could do was feel sick and blue, and that was between sessions of feeling like he had a hole blown in his guts.

Chapter 25

Beth hurried straight into her bedroom and shut the door. She didn't want Pa asking sarcastically how her day was, or Ma checking her over, either. She didn't want to think about today any more at all, but she caught her own eye in the dresser mirror, and turned sharply to confront herself. "Stupid, you queered it, didn't you." She pulled the pink dress off and tossed it on the bed where it subsided in a little heap that looked so sorry she poked a hanger into it and hanged it onto the closet pole next to the print outfit she'd worn for Bill's last night. It reminded her how Bill had kissed her goodbye, as if it mattered to him. She was plenty mad anyhow, but that made her madder than anything. It was perfectly safe for Bill to be tender once his bags were packed and his kid sister waiting out front in the car. Bill was good at keeping his distance. He always caught on quick to somebody's shortcomings and oddities, and then he would think he understood a person. He wasn't mean about it, just funny. She used to laugh at what he said and think he was wise. But she knew now that was no way to do. She wished she'd called him on it.

Another thing she was sore about was how nice she'd always acted to Bill, right to the end, no matter how he made her feel, exactly opposite to how she'd treated Irv. The way she told Irv about the baby couldn't have been any meaner if she set out to hurt him. She saw again how his face looked, astonished, like he'd been hit, and then with the hurt showing and finally, when she named Earl the father, as though he had to spit out something tainted. That was the way she felt now about Earl. He made her sick.

Bunch of shit-heels the whole lot, except Irv. He treated her better than anybody else ever did. On the island, he looked as happy as if he'd seen some kind of vision. No wonder she backed out of the deception. It sure was 'learn as you go,' in this world. Before yesterday her only thought was to get out of the fix she was in by any means she could. Then she couldn't do it. Maybe what she really believed was that Irv wouldn't walk out on her—when he had time to cool down, he would come back. She supposed that was foolish; forgiveness was something men were supposed to get, not give, but you couldn't be sure about Irv. Anyway, for some reason she felt better, like she was an idiot and didn't realize how bad off she was.

Suddenly she heard Ma screaming out back. She ran through the house and found her standing on a ladder that was leaned up against the wine vat, yelling "Frank! Frank!" down into it.

"Get down, Ma. Let me," she commanded, and when Ma got off the ladder, she raced up it. Pa was at the bottom of the vat sitting in mashed grapes almost up to his chin, with his legs straight out before him in the brown hip boots he always wore when he trod out the wine. He looked totally woozy, like he could keel over any second and drown in the purple mush.

"Hand me that lug box, Ma," she yelled. Liz reached the big box up to her, and she dropped it over the side, then let herself down beside her father. The sour, alcohol-tangy fumes were so powerful, she gasped and coughed and her eyes smarted and teared. No wonder Pa was just about out. He always joked about the free drunk he got from the fumes when he stamped the wine grapes, but they'd never been anything like this. This batch had fermented way too long. She held her breath all she could, and squinted her eyes while she stood the box on end, and got Pa to sit up on it, hauling him under the arms like a rag doll while she yelled at him to get his feet under him and help. He kept almost passing out as she braced him against the side of the tank wondering when the fumes would catch up with her. "I can't hold him, Ma," she hollered. "Get a rope."

Liz brought a clothesline and Beth got a loop of it around Frank under the arms while Liz knotted the other end to the railroad ties the vat sat on. Frank slumped into the support and Beth got up beside him on the box, wiggling her toes under him for a foothold and strained up so her head was over the top of the vat in the air. She was afraid the fumes would hurt the baby, they were so strong.

"It's poisonous down here, and I can't get him any higher. We've got to get help," she told her mother.

"Earl was here, but he went to Smith's." Beth said if Ma could keep Pa afloat with the rope, she would go get somebody in the truck. She pulled herself up till she could get one leg over the top, with the dried out porous wood scraping the skin under her knee raw. She was plastered all over with the muck of the crushed grapes, and the sour juice stung. Earl's truck careened into the driveway and drew up at the vat.

"What the Christ!" he said when he saw her. He jumped out of the truck and ran up the ladder.

"Get down under him, while I haul him up," he ordered Beth. She got her father by the knees and held as much of his weight as she could while Earl hoisted him up so his head was at the rim. Liz took up the slack on the rope and anchored it again. Earl leaned over into the tank trying to pull him out, but couldn't get under the weight right. "Lift him, dammit," he yelled.

"No, Beth, don't!" Liz screamed, "You'll hurt the baby." She grabbed the ladder and shook it as hard as she could. "You go in and get him, you big lard," she hollered.

In the vat Frank slowly lolled his head upright and glared at Beth, then he tilted it back to take deep drags of air.

Beth stripped as much of the stinking purple muck as she could off herself, and then started to get it off Pa. He turned himself away from her hands and let Earl grapple with him as he was.

While Liz hobbled Frank off to the bathtub, Earl climbed the ladder again and looked down at Beth.

"You want a hand?" he asked. Beth threw her scraped leg over the top again and pulled herself up.

"Just get off the ladder," she said.

She stayed in her room till Ma called her for dinner. Frank, in robe and slippers, watched her grimly over the rim of his wine glass as she helped Liz get the food on the table.

"It's Bill's, I suppose," he mused. "That explains why he cleared out of the county so fast, don't it." Beth, at the stove wheeled indignantly to face him but Frank refused to be interrupted. "Well you can write him I'm not paying for the abortion. Tell him from me that unless he gets the money to you in a week, I'm going to strike Wint up for it," he said, nodding his head righteously. His skin had a yellow waxy look that showed up the brown spots, and his gray streaked hair clung wet and flat to his head from his bath. For the first time, Beth realized he looked old. She almost felt sorry for him. "Oh Pa, calm down," she said wearily. "Bill's not the father and there's not going to be any abortion."

Who is then?" He jumped in, mid sentence, as though it were an argument he could win.

"Earl. Your big buddy." Her voice was vindictive.

"It's got to be my fault somehow, don't it?" Frank said. "Well then if its Earl's, he can pay to get rid of it."

"Why don't you listen to me, Pa. I said I'm not going to have an abortion." She'd never bucked Pa seriously before in her life. It gave her an odd feeling, like she was in a play about somebody else. And the strangest thing was she wanted to keep the baby, not because of Ma's church stuff about abortion or anything else, she just wanted it.

Frank turned his head away, dismissing the subject. "You're lucky it's Earl's. then," he said. "At least he'll marry you. I'll see to that."

"No you won't." Her voice punched him. "I wouldn't marry that crum for anything on earth."

"There aren't going to be any bastards in this house." He planted his knuckles on the couch, and pushed himself up heavily. Beth shrank away from him. He hadn't hit her since she was grown, but she wasn't counting on it. "You'll do as I say or this is the last meal you get here." He settled at the table.

Beth circled around it and sat down across from him with a huffy fling of her hip. If this was the last meal, she better eat it, since she didn't know where the next one was coming from. Her insides froze as she recognized the truth of the thought, so that she couldn't eat if she tried, but she messed around with her food and pretended to, like a kid. Then she said she was going to bed, she felt sick.

She heard Earl's truck the next morning when he picked Frank up for work. At supper time, she heard it stop on the far side of the road instead of coming into the yard as usual. She went to the front window to see why. They were busy unloading long two-by-fours under the trees beside the branch of the creek where it went under the road in a culvert. The stack they had started was on the spot Pa always said was the best building site on the place. With the long pieces of lumber stretching between them, they walked sideways smoothly, each crossing the same foot over the other in rhythm, talking and laughing easily, old teammates.

"Will you look at this, Ma?"

Liz came and stood beside her, watching. "I told you he was dead set on something when he went off this morning."

"What's he going to do, build a pen for me? He's crazy."

"No, but he's bullheaded and his temper's getting worse than ever. You won't cross him if you know what's good for you. Besides, if he's going to build you a house, it's hard to complain about that. I didn't think he had that much put by, but I guess he could have."

"Ma," Beth turned to look curiously at her mother, "you're talking as though I should marry that louse."

"You liked him well enough to get pregnant." Liz tilted her head to one side, and regarded Beth with a look that was guarded, speculative.

Beth watched her, searching for a hint of humor, sarcasm, anything that would change the meaning of her look, which was that she'd be lucky to get anybody at all to marry her. She had known Ma wouldn't fight Pa for her, but she never expected her to let her down in her heart like that.

"Who said I ever *liked* Earl?" She said this half under her breath, musing, as though she didn't have anybody else to talk to.

Chapter 26

Irv's body was wrenched with a great jerk when his alarm went off. He had slept miserably, his eyes felt bloated, and he ached. He rolled over and grappled the pillow into place over his head and tried to forget he was alive, but the whole mess seized him, and he began to go over it for the twentieth time. He had hardly believed it, even when she had spelled everything out like she did. No wonder her voice was queer, like she had to get it out though clenched teeth. He would have wanted to kill them.

He kept seeing how her face changed when she finally finished, how the harshness disappeared and she looked sad, like she was sorry he had to hear it.

He was late getting off to work. Speeding wasn't going to get him there on time, but it gave him some satisfaction. He slowed as he passed Beth's house, cringing, to remember how he had just let her out of the truck and gone off. He felt awful about that, but it didn't change the way he felt about her and Earl together. Hatred rose in his throat like vomit. And a little Earl? Christ, Beth!

Work was awful. They were stripping the trees, and that meant if there was a pear left on a tree, pick it. You'd think he could do that asleep, but he caught himself standing with his head tilted back staring up into a tree for minutes as if it presented a problem. He kept remembering Beth on the island, the way she looked, every move she made. Then something that had glimmered unfocused in the background in his mind all night suddenly sailed out into the open. "The rest wasn't fake." He could hear how she had said it, in the same flat tone, but what it meant was different from the way she sounded, because "the rest" meant what they had done, the way it had been. If that wasn't faked, it made anything else insignificant.

Jesus, he was dumb. All he wanted in the world was Beth, and all he could think of was Earl.

Beth had carved herself up to tell him the truth. She didn't have to tell him. She could have fooled him, easy.

Blindly, he circled a tree for the third time with his head tipped back on his neck. He was startled when he saw the boss coming toward him from the house. Was he going to get fired for goofing off already?

Looking serious, the super motioned Irv aside. Bill had just called him long distance with a message for Irv. His mother had had a stroke, and she was still in a bad way. The doctor wasn't sure whether she would be impaired or not. A neighbor had been helping her, but now had to go back to work. Bill had said Irv better get down there right away. The super added that if it would help, Irv could pick up his pay immediately.

When he got back to the Winton's, Pod said to throw his stuff in a bag and hurry, he'd drive him in to catch the 10:30 bus.

Irv just had time to buy an envelope from the post mistress, and scribble a note:

Dear Beth, I just got word my mother had a stroke and I have to go home. Please don't be mad at me for last night. I'll write when I can.

I love you,

Irv

He pushed his letter through the drop slot, and hurried after the Greyhound driver, who was lugging the mail sack out to the bus.

Beth stuck to her story that she was sick, and stayed in bed whenever Pa was home. Ma brought Irv's letter in to her bedroom when Frank brought it home with the mail that night. Beth tore it open.

"Irv's gone home," she told Liz. "His mother had a stroke."

When Liz brought Beth her dinner, she also brought her a message from Frank. "Your father says you're to get up tomorrow and go get the license whether you're sick or not. He says you and Earl have got to get married as soon as they'll let you."

Beth was enjoying her food. She licked a finger thoughtfully, "Can I get the license myself, or does Earl have to be there?"

"Earl says he'll take off tomorrow afternoon and pick you up at 2:00. You have to go to Lakeport for it."

Beth considered that for a minute, eyes on her empty plate.

"O.K.," she said cheerfully. "Any more ravioli?" Liz stood regarding her a moment, then nodded and took the plate to get her some more.

When she heard the men leave the next morning, Beth got out of bed and went to the kitchen in her robe and slippers for breakfast.

"You aren't really sick are you, Babe?" Liz asked.

"No, Ma, I'm not sick. I want to have a bath before I get dressed is all."

In her pink rayon slip and white-towel turban she slid back the curtain of her closet and dressed carefully, then packed as much as would go into her small suitcase. She made her bed and went back into the kitchen, holding the suitcase in front of her with both hands. "Goodbye Ma," she said, "I've got to go."

Liz eyed the suitcase, and nodded, her dark eyes heavy and sad. "What are you going to do, Babe?"

"I don't know for sure, but I sure am leaving!"

Liz took her in her big arms. Tears slowly found the best path down her face.

"Irv asked me to marry him Sunday, Ma, but I told him about the baby. It hit him hard. I don't know where we stand now." She gave a funny little shrug. "Maybe I can take care of his old lady."

Liz couldn't tell whether Beth was serious, or not, the way she had been acting lately.

"I know you don't want to go to any of the family," she told her, "but if you have to, go to your grandmother." Beth pressed her lips together to keep from crying and nodded.

She went out to the road. At least three farmers higher up the gulch took milk to the grocer every morning, so she was sure she would get a ride in the next half hour. She hoped it would be Wint, so he could tell her about Irv, but he wasn't the one who showed up first, and she couldn't risk waiting for him.

It was still before eight when she got to town. A few cars came through hurrying elsewhere. Gene Waukup was opening his grocery store. Mrs. Snook swept the sidewalk in front of the hotel. The rest of the town waited.

Charlie Norton's truck stood in front of the cafe. If Charlie was going to Hopland, he would take her. She studied the load that showed through the truck rails: bulging cardboard boxes, a suitcase, an axe, a shovel, a shotgun, a radio, and a ripped leather armchair. Comforts of home. It looked like Charlie was leaving town too.

He came out of the cafe with a steaming cup of coffee in his hands and stood taking the early sun with Harry in front of the barber shop. She went over to them, "Are you pulling out soon, Charlie? How about a ride?"

He glanced at her face, and at the small suitcase. "Sure thing," he said. "Just let me finish the Java."

He took his cup back to the counter inside. "O.K.," he said to Beth, emerging, "Let's hit it." He shoved her suitcase into the high cab.

Beth stared out the side window for a long time, tense and unseeing. The back of her head and cheek, twisted away from him, looked stubborn, sort of sulky. He let her be.

Finally outside of Lakeport, when they started up the grade, she began watching the road, and the scenery. He could see she was livening up. Her eyes sparkled with anticipation. He'd always thought Beth was a very pretty woman, but he'd never seen her look this good.

"You going down to the City?"

"Um hm," she said.

"Seems like half the people in the gulch are leaving this month, just like the fruit tramps. Going to your Ma's folks?"

"Mm—"

"Mm—" Charlie mocked. "What's up? Are you running?"

"Yes, I am."

"All right, so where are you going?" he asked again.

"I'm going to Oakland, Irv's mother's place."

"Irv left too, huh?"

"His mother had a stroke."

Charlie gave his head a single shake, and clicked his tongue at fate. "And what are you going to do when you get there?"

"You sure ask a lot of questions, Charlie. I'm going to marry Irv, I think."

Charlie studied her profile for as long as he could on that road. His guess was the little guy with the yellow hair must have got Beth pregnant, and Frank Hafner was pulling heavy-father stuff on her. Old Frank, more combustion than brains, like me. Izzy's pale little face floated before his eyes like gauze. That dumb-bastard Frank, he doesn't know how sorry he's going to be when he finds out his daughter's gone. He looked at Beth again. She was one pretty woman.

"I'll be damned," he said. "Why would you do that?"

Beth thought about it, her eyes on Charlie's face, but not seeing him. "Because he loves me, I suppose," she said finally.

"And do you love him," his tone mimicked hers.

She look at him coldly, and turned back to watching the bleached hills shoulder one another away as the truck circled another curve.

"I guess I don't know an awful lot about love," she answered. Mainly, I'm just leaving."

"That right?" he asked absently, as though he was just keeping the conversation going.

"What's all that stuff of yours in back for. It looks to me like you're leaving too."

"Well, actually, you caught me just in time. I'll be making the Ukiah run from now on, so I'm moving my stuff to Hinkley's Hopland Hotel." He drawled out the name to make it funny, but his thoughts were surly. Big change for me, too. I'll be driving up and down the coast, instead of over the grade and back, but still in Hinkley's rotten truck.

"You don't seem very enthusiastic about it," said Beth.

"Yeah, I am. I was." He quit talking. It had seemed like a good move, Gloria in her little edge-of-the-mountain house in Hopland, the new run, new terrain. Living at the old place was awful now, as though everybody had died, Stevie, Isobel, Viv, and especially, him. He couldn't stand to think about it.

"Well then, why are you running?"

Charlie didn't answer. He looked absorbed in maneuvering the truck around a small gray-brown carcass in the road.

THE END

About the Author

Phyllis Whetstone Taper was born in Santa Paula, California. In 1925 the family moved to the dry climate of a ranch in Lake County for her father's health (as a superintendent of a small insulation factory he was an early victim of asbestosis). There she studied piano with Corabelle Piner, who had retired to Lake County from The Piner Music school, and later at the Cora W. Jenkins music school in Piedmont, both on a work-for-lessons basis.

She received a small Lake County scholarship to the University of California, Berkeley, where she edited its literary magazine, The Occident, was elected to Phi Beta Kappa, graduated with honors in English, and married the editor of its humor magazine, The Pelican.

After WWII, her husband's work in the occupation government took them to Berlin and Stuttgardt, where their first child,was born. His identification tag at the foot of the bed, in military style read "Name: Philip Taper, Occupation: baby."

Years in New York City followed. When she was fifty she took a master's degree at Columbia University, and became an instructor at Drew University in New Jersey. When the family returned to Berkeley she joined Bob Gluck's group for older writers in San Francisco and was a member of the David R. Brower, Ronald Dellums Institute for Sustainable Policy Studies at Merritt College in Oakland.